"I Saw The Way You Were Looking At Me Just Now. It Isn't Too Late To Renegotiate, Jules."

The heat of his gaze instantly warmed the blood pumping through her veins. He very quickly made her aware of every inch of her body and how she responded to him.

"Yes it is," she said. "Way, way too late."

"Well then, I guess I'm just trying to be nice."

He made her reluctance to accept his offer seem childish. "Of course," she said, but a part of her still wondered. There were too many undercurrents running between their every interaction.

They had been apart for so long, most days it was easy to ignore what had happened between them. But now they were looking at months together. In close quarters.

Julianne had the feeling that the pressure cooker they'd kept sealed all this time was about to blow.

* * *

Her Secret Husband
is a Secrets of Eden story: Keeping their past buried isn't so easy when love is on the line.

* * *

If you're on Twitter,
tell us what you think of Harlequin Desire!
#harlequindesire

Dear Reader,

I know you've been waiting for this book to arrive. At least I hope so. I've been accused of torturing readers for nearly two years with the secrets that have carried through this miniseries. I've gotten numerous emails and messages asking, "When are we going to find out about the body?", "Why are there only four books? I want Julianne's story, too!", "I seriously have to wait a year to find out how it ends?" and "Did you really just kill Ken and end the book? Are you trying to give me a heart attack, too?"

My own mother cornered me in the kitchen once and insisted to know what was going on. I've been pretty tight-lipped about the whole thing, even lying by omission to avoid giving away spoilers. I didn't want to ruin the surprise. Well, my dear readers, the time has come. I promise that all will now be revealed!

When I was writing *Undeniable Demands,* the first book in the Secrets of Eden miniseries, I immediately fell in love with Heath. The moment he stepped onto the page with his charming smile and smart mouth, I was hooked. It also made me wonder what his humor was hiding. It turns out he was hiding quite a bit, if the title of this book is any indication. When Heath offered to kiss Tori under the mistletoe and Julianne threw an elbow in his ribs, I knew something was going on between him and the Edens' only daughter. In this book, I finally got the pleasure of uncovering their past and plotting their future.

If you enjoy Heath and Julianne's story, tell me by visiting my website at www.andrealaurence.com, like my fan page on Facebook or follow me on Twitter. I'd love to hear from you!

Enjoy,

Andrea

HER SECRET
HUSBAND

—

ANDREA LAURENCE

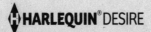

Recycling programs
for this product may
not exist in your area.

ISBN-13: 978-0-373-73345-3

Her Secret Husband

Printed in U.S.A.

ANDREA LAURENCE

is an award-winning contemporary romance author who has loved books and has been writing stories since she learned to read and write. She always dreamed of seeing her work in print and is thrilled to be able to share her books with the world. A dedicated West Coast girl transplanted into the Deep South, she's working on her own "happily ever after" with her boyfriend and five fur-babies. You can contact Andrea at her website, www.andrealaurence.com.

One

"Your dad's heart attack was pretty serious this time."

The doctor's words did little to make Heath Langston feel better about his foster father's condition. He stood outside Ken Eden's hospital room, listening to the doctor's prognosis. He felt helpless, which was not the way he liked it. He might be the youngest of the "Eden boys," but he owned his own advertising firm on Madison Avenue. He'd single-handedly developed one of the most successful ad campaigns of the last year. He was used to everyone, from his secretary to his business partner, looking to him to make decisions.

But this was serious stuff. Life and death. Not exactly his forte. Ken and Molly Eden's only biological child, Julianne, hadn't stopped crying since she arrived. Heath preferred to keep things light and he'd much rather see Julianne smile, but even he couldn't find anything to make a joke about right now.

The Edens' five children had rushed to their family farm in Cornwall, Connecticut, the moment they'd gotten the call about Ken's heart attack. Heath had gotten into his car and bolted from New York City, not knowing if his foster father would be alive by the time he got to the hospital. His biological parents had died in a car accident when he was only nine years old. He was a grown man now, the CEO of his own company, but he wasn't ready to face losing another parent.

Heath and Julianne were the last to arrive and were receiving the report the others had already heard.

"He's stable now, but we were lucky," the doctor continued. "That aspirin Molly gave him may have made all the difference."

Julianne's tiny figure stood in front of him. Despite the doctor's serious words, Heath couldn't keep his eyes from going to her. She took after Molly, being petite but powerful. Today, she looked even smaller than normal, with her shoulders hunched over and her head dipped down to focus her eyes on the floor. Her blond hair had been long and loose when she'd first arrived, but after sitting forever in the waiting room, she'd clipped it up into a messy twist. She shivered at the doctor's words and tried to snuggle deeper into her green cashmere sweater.

Heath put a reassuring hand on her shoulder. His brothers each had their fiancées to hold for support, but he and Julianne were both alone. His heart went out to her. He hated seeing his feisty, confident artist looking so broken. Although they'd grown up in the same house, she had never been a sister in his mind. She had been his best friend, his partner in crime, and for a short time, the love of his life.

Knowing they had each other in this dark moment made him feel better. Tonight, he hoped they could put their tumultuous past behind them and focus on what was more important. Since Julianne didn't pull away, she had to feel the same. Normally, she would give him a playful shove and artfully dodge the physical contact, but not today.

Instead, her body slumped against him for support, her back pressing into his chest. He rested his cheek against the gold strands of her hair and deeply breathed in the scent that was imprinted on his brain. She sighed, sending a tingle of awareness traveling along his spine. The sensation turned the doctor's voice into a muffled mutter in the distance. For a moment, there was only him and her. It wasn't the most appropriate of times, but he would revel in the contact.

Touching Julianne was a rare and precious experience. She had never been a very physically demonstrative person, unlike Molly, who hugged everyone she met, but she kept an even greater distance from Heath. No matter what had happened between them all those years ago and who was to blame, in a moment like this he regretted the loss of his best friend the most acutely.

"He's going to need open-heart surgery. After that, he'll have to stay in ICU a few days until we can move him to a regular room."

"How long until he'll be able to come home?" Julianne asked, making Heath feel guilty for where his mind had strayed. Even as they touched, she was focused on something more important than the two of them and their history together. It was enough for him to straighten up and put some distance between their bodies once again. He opted to focus on the doctor's answer instead.

The doctor frowned. "I don't like to set expectations on this kind of thing, but as I told the others, he's going to be with us a week at least. He might need to go into a rehab center for a while. Maybe he could be at home if there's a bed downstairs and a nurse could be brought in. After that, he's going to have to take it easy for a few months. No lifting, no climbing stairs. He won't be cutting down pine trees this Christmas, that's for sure."

That decided it. With everything else that was going on, Heath had already been thinking of taking a few months off to return to his foster parents' Christmas-tree farm. A body had been discovered on former family property last Christmas and it had recently been identified as Tommy Wilder, a foster child who had stayed briefly on the farm. Heath and the other Eden children knew that Tommy had been dead nearly sixteen years, but the police investigation was just now heating up.

Heath had been torn between wanting to keep up with every news story on television about Tommy and wishing he could just pretend the bully had never existed. Unfortunately, he knew well that ignoring issues wouldn't make them go away.

As much as he hated to admit it, it was time for Heath to come home and answer for what he'd done. It was just Ken and Molly on the farm now, and although they knew nothing about the truth behind Tommy's disappearance, they were having to deal with the police investigation on their own. According to his only biological brother, Xander, the stress of Sheriff Duke threatening to arrest Ken had put him into the hospital today.

It was bad enough that one person was dead because of Heath's mistakes. He couldn't bear it if someone else, especially someone innocent like Ken, also fell victim.

The doctor disappeared and he and Julianne made their way back to the waiting room area, where the rest of the family was assembled. His three brothers and their fiancées were scattered around the room. Some were reading magazines, others were focused on their phones. All looked tired and anxious. "I'll be coming to stay at the farm until Dad is better," he announced to the group. "I can handle things."

"I know it's only the beginning of October, but Christmas will be here before you know it," his oldest foster brother, Wade, pointed out with a frown furrowing his brow. "The last quarter of the year is always a nightmare. You can't take all that on by yourself."

"What choice do we have? All of you are busy. My business partner can run Langston Hamilton for a few months without me. And I've got Owen," Heath added, referring to the Garden of Eden Christmas Tree Farm's oldest and most faithful employee. "He can help me with the details. When Christmas comes, I'll hire some of the high school and college boys to bag and haul trees."

"I'm coming home, too," Julianne announced.

The whole family turned to look at her. She'd been fairly quiet since she had arrived from the Hamptons, but only Heath seemed to realize the significance of her decision. She was volunteering to come home, even knowing that Heath would be there. While she visited the farm from time to time, it was very rare that the boys were there aside from Christmas celebrations. Volunteering to spend months with Heath was out of character for her, but she wasn't exactly in a good headspace.

Despite how small and fragile she looked, there was a sternness in her eyes. Unfortunately, Heath knew that look well. The hard glint of determination, like emeralds, had set into her gaze, and he knew she wouldn't be dissuaded from her decision. Once Julianne's mind was made up about something, there was no changing it.

Even without Heath there, her coming to the farm was a big deal. Julianne was a sculptor. Both her studio and her boutique gallery were in the Hamptons. It wasn't the kind of job where you could just pick up your twelve-hundred-pound kiln and work wherever you like.

"What about your big gallery show next year?" Heath said. "You can't afford to lose two or three months of work to come down here."

"I'm looking to set up a new studio anyway," she said.

Heath frowned. Julianne had a studio in her home. The home she shared with her boyfriend of the last year and a half. It was a personal record for her and everyone thought Danny might be a keeper. Looking for a new studio meant looking for a new place to live. And possibly a new relationship.

"Has something happened with you and Danny?" their brother Brody asked, saving Heath the trouble of nosing into her love life.

Julianne frowned at Brody, and then glanced around at her protective older brothers with dismay. She obviously didn't want to talk about this now, or ever. "Danny and I are no longer 'Danny and I.' He moved out about a month ago. I needed a change of scenery, so I've sold the house and I'm looking for something new. There's no reason why I can't move back for a few months while Dad recuperates. I can help around the farm and work on my art pieces when we're closed. When Dad's feeling better, I'll look for a new place."

Heath and the other boys looked at her dubiously, which only made the color of irritation flush her pale, heart-shaped face. "What?" she said, her hands going to her hips.

"Why didn't you say anything about your breakup with Danny? And selling your house? You two were together a long time. That's a pretty big deal," Xander noted.

"Because," Julianne explained, "three of you guys have gotten engaged recently. It's bad enough that I'll be going stag to all of your weddings. I wasn't exactly looking forward to telling all of you that I've got yet another failed relationship under my belt. Apparently I'm doomed to be the old maid in the family."

"That's hardly possible, Jules," Heath said.

Julianne's cool, green gaze met his. "Point is," she continued, deliberately ignoring his words, "I'm able to come home and help, so I will."

Heath could tell by her tone that the discussion was over for now. Taking her cue, he turned to the rest of his siblings. "Visiting hours are about over, although you'll pay hell to get Mom from Dad's bedside. The rest of us probably need to say good-night and head back to the farm. It's been a long, stressful day."

They shuffled into Ken's hospital room, the dark, peaceful space ruined by the beep of Ken's heart monitor and the low rumble of the voices on his television. There was one light on over the bed, illuminating Ken's shape beneath the off-white blanket. He was nearly as pale as the sheets, but it was a big improvement over the blue-tinged hue his skin had taken on earlier. His light blond, nearly white hair was disheveled from constantly pulling out his oxygen tube and putting it over the top of his head like a pair of sunglasses. Molly had obviously forced it back into his nose recently.

She was sitting in a reclining chair beside him. It was the kind that extended into a bed and that was a good thing. Molly wasn't going anywhere tonight. Her normally cheery expression was still pasted onto her face, but that was more for Ken's benefit than anything. Heath could tell there wasn't much enthusiasm behind it. They were all struggling just to keep it together for Dad's sake.

Ken shifted his gaze from his favorite evening game show to the group of children huddled at his bedside. Heath realized they must look ridiculous standing there. Five rich, successful, powerful people moping at their father's hospital bed, unable to do anything to help. All their money combined couldn't buy Ken a new heart.

At least, not *legally*. Since they'd already done their fair share of dancing on the wrong side of the law and had enough police lurking around their property to prove it, they'd stick with the doctor's recommendations for now.

"There's not much happening here tonight," Ken said. He tried to cover the fact that speaking nearly winded him, but he had to bring his hand to his chest and take a deep breath before saying anything else. "You kids get on home and get some rest. I'll be here. I'm not going anywhere, anytime soon."

Julianne stepped to his side and scooped up his hand. She patted it gently, careful not to disturb his IV, and leaned in to put a kiss on his cheek. "Good night, Daddy. I love you."

"I love you too, June-bug."

She quickly turned on her heel and moved to the back of the group so others could take their turns. She'd let the tears on her cheeks dry, but Heath could see more threatening. She was trying to hold them in and not upset Ken.

One by one, the rest of them said good-night and made their way out to the parking lot. The hospital was a good distance from Cornwall, so they merged onto the highway and made the long, dark drive back to their parents' farm.

Wade and Tori returned to their nearby home, but the rest of the family continued on to the farm. The boys each parked at the bunkhouse, leaving an impressive display of luxury vehicles out front. Heath was last, pulling his Porsche 911 Carrera in between Xander's Lexus SUV and Brody's Mercedes sedan.

Twenty-five years ago, the old barn had been converted into a guest house of sorts, where the foster children who came to live at the Garden of Eden would stay. It had two large bedrooms and baths upstairs and a large common room with a small kitchenette downstairs. It was filled with old, but sturdy furniture and all the comforts teenage boys needed. Heath was the youngest of the four boys who had come to the farm and stayed until adulthood. These days they spent their time in multimillion-dollar mansions and apartments, but this farm was their home and when they returned, the boys always stayed in the bunkhouse.

Heath watched Julianne pull her red Camaro convertible up closer to the main house. The old Federal-style home was beautiful and historic, but it didn't have enough space for a large crew of children. Ken and Molly had a bedroom, their daughter, Julianne, had a room and there was one guest room.

She stood on the porch, fumbling with her keys and looking lost. Heath didn't like that at all. Normally, Julianne was a woman who knew exactly what she wanted from life and how to get it. But tonight she looked anything but her normally spunky self. Nearly losing Ken right after things went south with Danny must have been more than she could take.

Heath grabbed his overnight bag from the trunk of his Porsche and followed the group into the bunkhouse. He set his duffel bag on the old, worn dining room table and looked around. The downstairs common room hadn't changed much since he'd moved in, aside from the new flat-screen television Xander had purchased during his recent stay.

There was a sense of comfort in being back home with his family. He imagined that wouldn't be the same for Julianne, who would be returning to an empty house. Heath might not be the person she'd choose to stay with her tonight, but he wasn't going to argue with her about it. He wasn't leaving her alone.

"Hey, guys," he said to his brothers and their fiancées as they settled in. "I think I'm going to sleep in the big house tonight. I don't like the idea of Jules being alone. Not after the day we've had."

Xander nodded and patted him on the shoulder. "That's a good idea. We'll see you in the morning."

Heath picked up his bag, stepped out and then jogged across the grass and gravel to the back door.

Julianne knew she should go to bed; it had been a very long day with unexpected twists and turns, but she wasn't sleepy. She'd woken up worried about her work and the fallout of her latest failed relationship. Then the phone rang and her world turned upside down. Her previous worries were suddenly insignificant. She'd dropped everything, thrown some clothes in a bag and hit the road.

Even now, hours later, she was still filled with nervous energy. There was a restless anxiety in her muscles, the kind that urged her to go to her workshop and lose herself in the clay. Usually, immersing herself in her work helped clear mind and solve her problems, but all the pottery in the world wouldn't fix this.

She settled for a cup of chamomile tea at the kitchen table. That might bring her brain down a few notches so she could sleep. She was sitting at the table, sipping the hot tea, when she heard a soft tap at the door. The door almost immediately opened and before she could get up, Heath was standing in the kitchen.

"What is it?" she said, leaping to her feet. "Did the hospital call? Is there a problem?"

Heath frantically shook his head, making one curl of his light brown hair dip down into his eyes. He held up his hands in surrender and she noticed the duffel bag on his shoulder. "No, no problem. Dad's fine," he insisted. "I just didn't want you to be alone in the house tonight."

The air rushed out of her lungs in a loud burst. Thank goodness Dad was okay. Her heart was still racing in her chest from her sudden panic as she slipped back down into her chair. She took a large sip of the scalding tea and winced. After the day she'd had, she didn't need Heath hovering nearby and the distracting hum of his presence in her veins. An hour after they had left the hospital, she could still recall the weight of his hand on her shoulder and the comforting warmth of his chest pressed against her. The contact had been innocent, but her eyes had fluttered closed for a moment to soak in the forbidden contact. She'd immediately snapped herself out of it and tried to focus on her father's health.

"I'll be okay alone," she said.

Heath dropped his bag onto the wooden floor and flopped in the chair across from her. "No, you won't."

She sighed and pinched the bridge of her nose between her thumb and middle finger. She could feel a headache coming on and that was the last thing she needed. Of course, she could take one of her migraine pills and knock herself out. That was one sure way to get to sleep tonight, but what if something happened to Dad?

When she looked up at her guest, she found herself getting lost in the light hazel depths of his eyes. Heath was always happy, always ready with a joke or a smile. But tonight, his expression was different. There was a softness, a weariness, that lined his eyes. He looked concerned. Worried. But not for Ken. At least not entirely. He was concerned about her.

As always.

Julianne wouldn't make light, even in her own mind,

of Heath's protectiveness of her. He had gone to extraordinary lengths to keep her safe. She knew that anytime, day or night, she could call him and he would be there. But not just because they were family and he cared about her. There was a great deal more to it than that and tonight was not the night she was willing to deal with it.

"Thank you," she said at last. She wasn't going to put up a fight and force him into the bunkhouse. She didn't have the energy to argue and frankly, it would be nice to have someone in the big, creaky house with her. No matter what had happened between them over the years, she always knew she could count on him to respect her boundaries.

"It feels weird to be in the house without Mom and Dad," he said, looking around at the large, empty kitchen. "Mom should be fussing at the sink. Dad should be tinkering with farm equipment outside."

He was right, but she didn't want to think about things like that. Those thoughts would require her to face the mortality of her aging parents. Dad would come home this time, but eventually, he wouldn't. She'd rather pretend they were immortal, like she had believed as a child. "Would you like some tea?" she asked, ignoring his words.

"No, I'm fine, thanks."

She wished he would have accepted the tea. That would have given her something to do for a couple of minutes. Instead, she had to sit idly and wait for the questions she knew were coming. They hadn't been alone together and able to really talk since before she had left for college eleven years ago. That had been by design on her part. There were so many thoughts, so many feelings she didn't want to deal with. Looking into Heath's eyes brought everything back to the surface. The burning attraction, the anxiety, the overwhelming feeling of fear…

"So, what happened with you and Danny? That seemed kind of sudden."

Julianne sighed. "We decided we wanted different things, that's all. I wanted to focus on my art and building my career. Things have really taken off and I want to strike while the iron is hot. Danny wanted to take our relationship to the next level."

A spark of interest flickered in Heath's light eyes, his full lips pursing with suppressed amusement. "He proposed?"

"Yes," she said, trying not to let the memories of the uncomfortable moment flood into her mind. She'd told him repeatedly that she wasn't interested in marriage right now, and kids were far, far on the horizon. And yet he'd asked anyway. He seemed to mistake her hesitation as her playing hard to get or using reverse psychology with him. She wished she knew why. She'd given him no signals otherwise. "I refused, as politely as I could, but he didn't take the rejection very well. After that, we decided if we weren't moving forward, we were stagnating. So he moved out."

Danny had been a great guy. He was fun and exciting and sexy. At first, he hadn't seemed interested in settling down. Given her situation, he was the perfect choice. She didn't want to get too serious, either. They wouldn't have even moved in together if he hadn't needed a new place on short notice. He must have seen that as a positive relationship step, when in fact it was simply practicality and economics. In time, it was just easier to stay together than to break things off and cause an upheaval.

"You didn't want to marry him?" Heath asked.

Julianne looked up at him again and shook her head in exasperation. That was a ridiculous question. He knew full well why she'd turned him down. "No, I didn't. But even if I *did*, what was I going to say to him, Heath?"

There was a long, awkward silence before Heath spoke again. "Jules?"

"Listen, I know I brought it up, but I really don't want to talk about it tonight." Julianne sipped the last of her tea and got up from the table. "With Dad and the stuff with Tommy, I can't take any more drama."

"That's fine," he said as he leaned back into the wooden chair and watched her walk into the kitchen. "But considering we're going to be spending the next few months together, you need to come to terms with the fact that we need to talk about it. We've swept the issue under the rug for far too long."

She knew when she made the decision to come home that this would happen. No matter how uncomfortable it might be, she knew they needed her help on the farm, so that was where she would be. There wasn't anywhere else for her anyway. She had sold her house. Closing was next week, and then she was officially homeless. She had to come back here. And she had to deal with her past once and for all.

Julianne looked over at the funny, charming man that had stolen her heart when she was too young and messed up to know what to do about it. Even now, the soft curve of his lips was enough to make a heat surge through her veins and a longing ache in her belly. It took almost no effort at all to remember how it felt when he'd kissed her the first time in Paris. The whisper of his lips along her neck as they admired the Sagrada Família in Barcelona...

Her parents thought they were sending their two youngest children on an exciting graduation trip through Europe. Little did they know what freedom and romantic settings would ignite between their daughter and their youngest foster child. Heath wasn't her brother. She'd known him before his parents died and had never thought of him like a brother. He was her best friend. But if she ever wanted him to be something more, she had to deal with the past.

"Agreed," she said. "Once Dad is stable and we have some time alone to talk, I'm ready to deal with it."

Heath narrowed his gaze at her and she knew instantly what he was thinking. He didn't believe her. She'd been feeding him excuses and dragging her feet for years. He probably thought she got some sort of sick pleasure from drawing all this out, but that was anything but true. She was stuck between not wanting to lose him and not knowing what do with Heath if she had him.

A lifetime ago, when they were eighteen and far, far from home, he'd wanted her. And she'd wanted him. At least, she thought she had. She was young and naive. Despite the attraction that burned at her cheeks when he touched her, she'd found she couldn't fully give herself to him in the heat of the moment.

"It's been easy to ignore while both of us were in school and building our careers," Heath said. "But it's time. Your recent breakup is one of several signs we can't disregard any longer. Whether you like it or not, eventually you and I are going to have to face the fact that we're still married."

Two

He'd laid his cards out on the table. This would end, and soon. After several minutes spent in silence, waiting for her to respond to his declaration, Heath finally gave up. "Good night, Jules," he said, pushing up from his seat.

With Ken's attack, he understood if she couldn't deal with this tonight, but he wasn't waiting forever for her. He'd already wasted too much time on Julianne. He picked his bag up off the floor, and carried it down the hall and up the stairs to the guest bedroom.

The guest room was directly across the hall from Julianne's room and next to the bathroom they would share. He could count on one hand how many times he'd slept in the big house over the years. It just wasn't where he was drawn to. The big house was beautiful and historic, filled with antiques and cherished knickknacks. Most anyone would be happy to stay here, but Heath always felt like a bull in a china shop when he was in the house.

As kids, the bunkhouse was the ideal boy zone. They could be rowdy because the furniture was sturdy but old, there were no breakable antiques and downstairs was all wood flooring, so they could spill and not stain the carpet. There was a big television, video games, a foosball table and an inexhaustible supply of soda and other snacks to fuel growing boys. Things had changed over the years, but being there with his brothers again would make it feel just the same.

Tonight, he made an exception and would stay in the big house for Julianne's sake, but it would be a mistake for her to confuse his gesture as weakness where she was concerned. Any love he had for her had fizzled away when she'd slammed her dorm room door in his face.

For years, he'd been as patient as he could stand to be. He knew now that he had been too nice. He'd given her too much space and let her get too contented. There was no incentive for her to act. That was going to change. He had no intention of being easy on her while they were here. Whatever it took, no matter how hard he had to push her out of her comfort zone, he would leave this farm a happily divorced man. Heath knew he shouldn't enjoy watching Julianne squirm, especially tonight, but he did.

Eleven years of marriage without his wife in his bed could do that to a guy.

He opened the door to the guest room and put his bag down on the white eyelet bedspread. The room was intricately decorated, like the rest of the house, with antique furniture, busy floral wallpaper, lacy curtains and shelves filled with books and framed pictures. As he kicked out of his Pràda loafers, he noticed a portrait on the wall in a carved, wooden frame.

It was of Julianne. One of her elementary school pictures, although he couldn't be sure what year. Her golden hair was pulled up into a ponytail, a sprinkle of freckles across her nose. She was wearing a pink plaid romper with a white turtleneck underneath it. She looked just as he remembered her.

He had fallen in love with Julianne Eden the first time he'd seen her. They were in Mrs. Henderson's fourth-grade class together. The cheerful blonde with the curly pigtails and the bright smile had sat right next to him. Whenever he forgot his pencil, she would loan him one of hers. They were pink and smelled like strawberries, but he didn't care. He left his pencil at home on purpose just so he could talk to her.

He'd fabricated childish plans to marry Julianne one day. It seemed like a pipe dream at the time, but one day on the playground, she kissed him—his very first kiss— and he *knew* that she was meant to be his. He'd even made her a Valentine's Day card to tell her how he felt.

He never gave her the card. The weekend before their class party, his parents were killed in a car accident. Heath had been in the car at the time, but his injuries, while serious, had not been fatal. When he was finally discharged from the hospital, both he and his brother, Xander, had found themselves in the care of Family Services. The next thing he knew, they were living at the Christmas-tree farm on the edge of town and the beautiful golden-haired girl of his dreams was supposed to be his "sister."

He had outright rejected that idea right away. They might live in the same home, but not once in twenty years had he ever referred to her as "sis" or "my sister." She was Jules, usually; Julianne when he was speaking about her to the uninitiated.

He'd given up the dream of ever marrying his child-hood love soon after coming to the Garden of Eden. Julianne never kissed him on the playground again. They were friends, but that was all. It wasn't until they were seniors in high school and the only kids left on the farm that things started to change between them. The trip to Europe had been the tipping point. Unfortunately, it hadn't tipped in his favor for long.

That seemed to be Julianne's M.O. Since they'd broken up, she had dated, but from what he could tell, never seriously and never for long. None of the brothers had ever met a boyfriend. She never brought one home to the farm. Danny had come the furthest, moving in with Julianne. She didn't really let any man get close, but Heath wasn't certain what was the cause and what was the effect. Did their marriage fail because she didn't do relationships, or did her relationships fail because she was married?

He had unpacked a few things and was halfway undressed when he heard a soft tap at his door. "Come in," he called out.

Julianne opened the door and stuck her head in. She started to speak, and then stopped, her gaze dropping from his face to his bare chest. He tried not to move, fighting the urge to puff up his chest and suck in his stomach. He liked to think he looked pretty good without all that, but it was such a reflex. He jogged the High Line every morning and lifted weights. As a child, he was always the smaller, scrappier of the boys, but no longer. He might be the shortest, at six feet, but he could take any of his brothers and look good doing it.

The dumbstruck Julianne seemed to agree. A crimson flush rose to her delicate, porcelain cheeks. Her full bottom lip hung, useless, until her tongue shot across it and her mouth slammed shut.

If Heath had known strutting around shirtless would get this kind of reaction from her, he would have done it a long time ago. Nothing made her more uncomfortable than the topic of sex. If he'd pushed the issue, perhaps he'd be happily single or happily married right now. Watching her reaction, he thrust his hands in his pockets. His Dolce & Gabbana slacks rode lower with the movement, exposing the trail of hair beneath his navel and the cut of his muscles across his hips.

Julianne swallowed hard and then shook her head and shifted her gaze away to the nearby armoire. "I'm s-sorry," she stuttered. "I didn't realize you were..."

"It's okay," Heath said with a sly smile, enjoying her discomfort. "I'm not bashful and it's nothing you haven't seen before."

She shook her head, sending a wave of the luxurious golden strands over her shoulders. "I don't remember you looking like *that*," she said, quickly bringing her hand up to cover her mouth. She looked embarrassed to share her observation aloud.

Heath glanced down at the display of his own body and shrugged. "I'm not eighteen anymore."

He supposed he would be struck just as hard to see her topless after all this time. Hell, he'd barely seen her naked back then. Sometimes when he was feeling particularly masochistic, he would allow himself to imagine what she looked like now beneath her sweaters and her jeans. The teenage girl he loved had become a very sexy and gifted woman. Any gangliness had been replaced with lush curves and soft, graceful movements. Beautiful and aggravating.

She stood awkwardly in the doorway, nodding, not looking at him, not saying anything for a few moments.

"Did you need something?" Heath prompted at last.

Her green gaze shifted back to his, her purpose suddenly regained. "Yes. Well, I mean, no. I don't *need* anything. I, uh, just wanted to say thank you."

"Thank you? For what?"

"For staying here with me tonight. I know you'd rather be laughing and chatting with Xander and Brody. You guys never get to see one another."

"I see them more than I get to see you," Heath said before he could stop himself. It was true. As children, they had been inseparable. She was his best friend. The marriage that should have brought them even closer together had driven them apart and he still didn't understand why. "I miss you, Jules."

A sadness crept into her eyes, a frown pulling down the corners of her mouth. "I miss you, too, Heath."

"Be honest. You avoid me. Why?" he asked. "Even if we divorced, I get the feeling that you'd still be uncomfortable around me."

"I'm not uncomfortable," she said, but not convincingly.

"Am I being punished for what happened between us?"

Julianne sighed and slumped against the door frame. "It's not about punishing you. And no, it's not about what happened in Europe, either. There are just things in our past that I don't like thinking about. It's easier to forget when I don't see or talk to you."

"Things in our past? Wait…" he said. "Are you blaming me for what happened with Tommy Wilder?"

"No!" she spoke emphatically, raising her palm up to halt him. "You are my savior. The one who protected me when no one else could."

"But you think of that horrible night when you look at me?" Heath was almost nauseated at the thought.

"No," she insisted again, but less forcefully. "If that were true, I never could've fallen for you. It's just easier for me to focus on the future instead of dwelling in the past. Our relationship is in my past."

"Not according to the public records office. It is very

much current and relevant. Ignoring things won't change them. It just makes it worse."

Julianne chuckled and crossed her arms over her chest. "Believe me, I know. I just don't know what else to do about it."

"We get divorced. We can't just stay married forever."

"It's worked okay so far."

Now it was Heath's turn to laugh. "Says the woman that just broke up with her boyfriend when he proposed."

"I didn't…" she began to argue, and then stopped. "This conversation has strayed from what I'd intended when I knocked. Thank you, again," she repeated. "And good night."

Heath watched her slip through the doorway. "Good night," he replied just as the door shut. Once he was certain she was settled in her room, he cast off the rest of his clothes and crawled into bed in his boxer shorts. The bed was soft and inviting, the sheets smelling like the lavender soap Molly used for linens and towels. The bed very nearly forced him to relax, luring him to the edge of sleep faster than he ever thought possible.

Things hadn't worked out between him and Julianne, but he wasn't stupid. He had long ago set aside any idea that their farce of a marriage might become something real. They'd never even consummated it. He'd thought she would come around eventually. It was her first time, perhaps she was just nervous. But then she left for her art program in Chicago without even saying goodbye. He chased after her, driving all night to figure out what was going on. He'd imagined a romantic moment, but instead, she'd told him their marriage was a mistake, he needed to forget it ever happened and practically shut her dorm room door in his face.

He'd been devastated. Then the devastation morphed

into anger. Then indifference. After that, he'd decided that if she wanted a divorce so badly, she could be the one to file. So he'd waited.

Eleven years.

As she'd mentioned, it hadn't been a problem. At least, logistically. He hadn't met a single woman that made him want to walk down the aisle again, but it was the principle of the thing. She didn't want him, and yet she was resistant to let him go. Julianne always seemed to have an excuse. They were broke. They moved around too much after school to establish residency. They were busy starting their businesses. Her appointment with her divorce attorney was rescheduled, and then rescheduled again.

After a while, he began to wonder if she would rather stay married and keep it a secret than file for divorce and risk people finding out she'd married *him*. Her big mistake.

He'd known her since they were nine years old and he still didn't understand what went on in that beautiful blond head of hers.

Julianne sat in a rocking chair on the back porch clutching a big mug of steaming coffee. She had barely slept last night and she desperately needed the infusion of caffeine to make it through today. She'd lain in bed most of the night thinking about Heath and how he was so close by. Her mind had wandered to their first trip together and how wonderful it had been. Even as young as they were, he'd known just how to touch her. With the backdrop of Europe, so romantic and inspiring, behind them, she thought she might be able to overcome the fear. She'd been wrong.

The familiar ache of need had curled in her belly, but she'd smothered her face in the pillows until it faded. It didn't matter how much she'd loved him back then. How much she wanted him. It didn't stop the fear from nearly strangling her with irrational panic. If she couldn't give herself to Heath, the one who protected her, the one she was closer to than anyone else… When it came down to it, she had been too messed up back then to be with anyone.

Heath was right, though. They needed to move on. She'd dragged her feet. Hoping the words would come easier after all this time, she made excuses. If the years had taught her anything, it was that the truth could be more painful than a lie. She lied for everyone's sake, including her own. To have a real, honest relationship with Heath, she would have to tell him the truth about their wedding night. And she just couldn't do it.

That meant that all there was left to do now was clean up the tattered remains of their relationship.

And there would be time for that soon. Other more pressing issues had to be addressed first, like arranging her move and seeing her father through his heart surgery, but even those could wait until after she'd had her coffee and settled into her day. It was early. The sun had just come up. Heath was still asleep and there was no sign of life from the bunkhouse. For now, it was just her, the cool air and the pine forest that spread out in front of her.

At one time in her life, those trees had been her sanctuary. Whenever something was troubling her, she could walk through row after row, losing herself in them. And then Tommy Wilder came to the farm. She never imagined someone could hurt her so badly and not kill her. The physical scars healed, but the emotional ones lingered. The trees had turned their backs on her that day, and she'd refused to go out there any longer. The boys had gladly picked up her share of chores in the field and she took on more responsibility in Molly's Christmas store. Her mother thought that it was Julianne's budding artistic spirit that drove her out of the trees and into the shop.

That was so far from the truth. It was actually the other way around. Her refuge in the shop had fueled an artistic creativity in her she didn't know she had. She started helping Molly decorate and make wreaths, but soon she was painting the windows and molding Nativity scenes out of clay. She was keeping so many painful, confusing things inside; it was easy to give her mind over to the intricacies of her art. It was only her good fortune that she was talented at what she did and was able to turn her therapy into a career.

The rumble of car tires across the gravel caught her attention. A moment later, Molly's Buick rounded the house and parked beside her Camaro.

Julianne got up and walked to the stairs to meet her. "Morning, Mama. Is Daddy doing okay?"

Molly nodded. "He's fine. Feeling well enough to shoo me home for a while. His surgery is tomorrow morning, so he wants me to take a break now, while I can."

That sounded like Daddy. He hated to be fussed over, just like she did. "I've made some coffee."

"Thank goodness," Molly said, slowly climbing up the stairs. "That sludge at the hospital hardly qualified."

They went inside and Julianne poured her a large mug with a splash of cream and one spoon of sugar. She joined her mother at the kitchen table, where she and Heath had had their uncomfortable conversation the night before. Looking at the weary, worn-out woman across from her, Julianne knew she just couldn't let her parents find out she'd eloped with Heath right out of high school.

It wasn't because of *whom* had she married, or even *how*. If Julianne hadn't been such a mess and things worked out, Molly wouldn't have been happy about them eloping, but she would have come around. The problem was explaining what went wrong between them and why she wasn't willing to work things out. Everyone would want to know how they could marry and break up in an instant. She couldn't even tell *Heath* that. How could she tell her parents, who had no clue that Tommy had ever laid a hand on her, much less ruined their daughter?

Julianne refused to be anything other than the cool and confident daughter of Ken and Molly. She supposed it was growing up as the only child of parents who desperately wanted more children. They loved her without question, but at the same time, they were always vocal about their disappointment in having only one. When they started taking in foster children, it made it even harder to get attention. At first, she tried to excel in school to prove to them that she was good enough to make up for being the only one. She was well-behaved, polite and never caused the tiniest problem for her parents.

It had worked. To a point. They were always quick to praise her, but her parents continued to bring in foster children. Perfection became her way to stand out and get noticed. It wasn't until after the incident with Tommy that she threw an uncharacteristic fit and demanded her parents stop bringing in other children and pay attention to her for once. It was selfish. And she felt horrible doing it. But she couldn't risk another boy coming to the Garden of Eden who might look at her the way Tommy did.

"Are you doing okay this morning?" Molly asked her.

"Yeah. Heath stayed in the guest room so I wouldn't be alone. We talked last night and a couple of us are going to come stay here for a few months. Through the New Year, at least, to help with Christmas and such."

Molly's chin shot up—her mother was ready to argue—but she stopped herself and nodded. They both knew she couldn't run the farm alone. Her petite frame and increasingly stiff fingers couldn't haul Christmas trees twice her size. Having the kids here would take the pressure off of her and keep Ken resting the way he should. "Which of you are coming up?"

"Heath and I. He's taking a few months away from the advertising agency. I've sold my house in Sag Harbor and I'm moving here until Dad is better, then I'll find someplace new."

"What about you and, uh…" Molly's voice trailed off.

Her mother couldn't remember the name of her boyfriend. That said volumes about her ill-fated relationship history. "Danny," Julianne offered. "We've broken it off."

"Oh," Molly said. "I'm sorry to hear that."

"Liar," Julianne said, smiling into her coffee mug as she took a sip.

Molly shrugged, but didn't argue with her on that point. "I've been speaking with a private medical care company about bringing your father home to recuperate instead of putting him in a nursing home. They recommended moving a bed downstairs, and they could provide a live-in nurse for a few weeks."

"That sounds perfect." She wanted her father to have the best possible care, but she hated the idea of him in a nursing home, even if temporarily.

"Well, except that you'd have to stay in the bunkhouse. We'd need to move one bed downstairs and have the other for the nurse. Is that okay?"

"Absolutely," Julianne responded, although the idea of close quarters with Heath didn't thrill her. Last night was bad enough. "It will give me some room to store my equipment, too."

"Speaking of which, what about your studio? And your gallery showing? You have to keep working, don't you?"

"The store is fine without me. My place in the Hamptons does too well to move and my staff there run it beautifully. As for my studio, I'm thinking I can work here and it wouldn't impact the show. Since I'm staying out there, maybe I can use part of the bunkhouse."

"You know," Molly said, "the storage room there hasn't been used in ages. We could clean that out and you could use it."

"Storage room?"

"Yes. You know what I'm talking about. In the bunkhouse, under the staircase. It's about twelve by twelve, I'd say, with a window and its own door to the outside. That's where we used to hide your Christmas presents when you all were small. Right now, I think it might just have some boxes of the boys' old toys and sporting equipment."

Honestly, she hadn't given much thought to the nook under the stairs. Her time in the bunkhouse was usually spent watching television or messing around with the boys, not surveying the property. "Now I remember. If it's as big as you say, that would be perfect."

"If Heath is staying," Molly continued, "perhaps he can help you get the space ready. There should be some time before the holiday rush begins."

"What am I helping out with?" Heath stumbled sleepily into the kitchen in jeans, a casual T-shirt and bare feet. His light brown hair was tousled. It was a far cry from his expensive tailored suits and perfectly styled hair, but it impacted Julianne even more powerfully. This morning, he looked more like the Heath she'd fallen in love with. The successful, powerful advertising executive was a stranger to her.

"We need you to help clean out the old storage room in the bunkhouse," Molly answered.

He located a mug and made his own cup of coffee. "The one where you hid our Christmas presents?"

A light flush of irritation rose to Molly's cheeks. Julianne had her mother's same pale, flawless complexion. It was always quick to betray their feelings. They blushed bright red at the slightest provocation.

"You knew about that?" Molly asked.

Heath smiled and took a step farther from his mother under the guise of looking in the cabinet for something to eat. "We've always known, Mom. We just didn't have the heart to tell you."

"Well, hell," Molly said, smacking her palm against the table. "Just as well we turn it into a studio, then."

"Mom says that Dad's surgery is tomorrow," Julianne added, steering the conversation in another direction.

Heath pulled down a box of cereal and nodded. "Once we're certain that he's doing okay after surgery, I'll probably head back to New York for a few days and get my things. I need to make arrangements with work and such, but I can probably be back up here in two or three days."

Julianne nodded. She had plenty of things to take care of, too. "Same here. I've got to close on the house. Most of my things are already boxed up. I'll put what I can in storage somewhere and bring the rest."

"How are you going to get all your stuff into that little bitty sports car?" Heath asked.

"The Camaro is bigger than your Porsche," she countered.

"Yeah, but I'm not hauling all your sculpting supplies and tools. What about your kiln?"

"I'm selling it locally," Julianne said, although she didn't know why he was so concerned. "I wanted a new one anyway, so I'll get it delivered here."

Heath frowned at her and crossed his arms over his chest in irritation. She tried not to focus on the way the tight fabric stretched across his hard muscles when he moved, but her eyes were instantly drawn to it. She followed the line of his collar to the lean cords of his neck and the rough stubble along his jaw. Her gaze stopped short when she noticed his amused smirk and arched eyebrow. He'd caught her. At that, she turned her attention back to her coffee and silently cursed herself.

"You need movers," he persisted. "And a truck. I can get you one."

Julianne scoffed at the suggestion. This was so typical of the way the last few years had gone. They avoided the big issues in their relationship and ended up quibbling about stupid things like moving trucks. She supposed to others, they seemed like bickering siblings, when in fact they were a grumpy, married couple. "I might need a truck, but I don't need you to pay for it. I'm capable of handling all that myself."

"Why won't you—"

"We'll discuss it later," she interrupted. She wasn't going to argue with him in front of Molly. She eyed her mother, who was casually sipping her coffee and sorting through her mail.

As if she could feel the tension in the room, Molly set down her stack of bills and stood up. "I'm going to go take a shower," she announced. She took the last sip of her coffee and went upstairs, leaving the two of them alone.

Heath took Molly's seat with a bowl of cereal in one hand and a mug of coffee in the other. "It's later."

"You paying for my movers looks suspicious," she complained. And it did. She made decent money. She didn't need someone to handle it for her, especially Heath playing knight in shining armor.

"I wasn't planning on paying for it. My agency handles the Movers Express account. The CEO owes me a favor. I just have to make a call. Any why is it suspicious? If Wade or Xander offered the same thing, you'd take them up on it without question."

"Because I understand their motives," Julianne said.

Heath's brows went up in surprise. "And what are my motives, Jules? Do you think I'll demand my rights as a husband in exchange for it? Sex for a moving truck? That's certainly a new one on me. Shoot. I should have made that part of the deal up front." His light hazel eyes raked over her, a devious smile curling his lips. He leaned across the table and spoke in a low, seductive tone. "I saw the way you were looking at me just now. It isn't too late to rene-gotiate, Jules."

The heat of his gaze instantly warmed the blood pump-ing through her veins. He very quickly made her aware of every inch of her body and how she responded to him. She wished he didn't have that power over her, but the moment she'd looked at him as something more than a friend, it was like a switch had flipped and she hadn't been able to reverse it. She also hadn't been able to do anything about the attraction.

"Yes, it is," she said, dropping her gaze to her coffee mug in the hopes she could suppress her stirring libido. "Way, way too late."

"Well then, I guess I'm just trying to be nice."

He made her reluctance to accept his offer seem child-ish. "Of course," she said, but a part of her still wondered. There were too many undercurrents running between their every interaction. Whenever Heath was nice to her, when-ever he did something for her, she couldn't help but won-der why. He had every reason to be angry with her. She'd treated him terribly, practically throwing his love back in his face.

On their trip to Europe, they had lain on the grass at the base of the Eiffel Tower and watched the lights twinkling on the hour. There, he'd confessed to her that he had been in love with her since the fourth grade. Swept up in the moment, she told him that she loved him, too. Their relationship had begun in Paris. The marriage started and ended in Gibraltar just three days later. She'd pushed him away for his own good, but he'd never understand that. All he saw was that she turned her back on him and wouldn't tell him why.

For a while he was angry with her. He didn't talk to her for their entire freshman year of college. Then he avoided her, doing internships instead of coming home for the summer. Their interactions were short, but polite. It took years, but eventually, he went back to the funny, easygoing Heath she'd always loved.

The light banter and humor covered up their issues, however. They had both been apart for so long, most days it was easy to ignore what happened between them on the graduation trip. But now they were looking at months together. In close quarters.

Julianne had the feeling that the pressure cooker they'd kept sealed all this time was about to blow.

Three

Ken's surgery went perfectly the next day. He spent twenty-four hours in ICU, and then he was moved to a regular room. Once he was off the ventilator and able to talk, Ken demanded everyone go home and stop hovering over him like it was his deathbed.

As instructed, Brody and his fiancée, Samantha, drove back to Boston. When Ken had his attack, Xander had been in Cornwall to move his ten-year-old son and new fiancée, Rose, to D.C. to live with him. He'd sent them along without him, so he gathered up the last of their things and met up with them back in D.C. Wade and Tori lived nearby and agreed to watch the farm while Heath and Julianne went home to make arrangements and make the transition to their new, temporary home.

Heath had offered to drive with Julianne and help with her move, but of course, she'd declined. He didn't know if she just didn't trust him, or if she felt too guilty to accept things from him after she'd broken up with him. He liked to think it was guilt.

The drive to Manhattan was quick, about two and a half hours. He called his business partner as he reached Chelsea and asked Nolan to meet him at his place to go over details while he packed. He found a metered spot on the street as he got off the phone. It was a great spot, considering how much he needed to load into the car. Some days he wasn't so lucky and wished he'd gotten a place with parking.

He hadn't been looking for a condo in this area when he first started shopping, but he'd fallen in love with the modern feel and large rooftop terrace that was bigger than his first New York apartment. Everything else, including parking, fell to the wayside. It was close enough to the office, near a subway stop and one of his favorite restaurants was a block up the street. He couldn't pass it up.

Heath had cleaned all the perishables out of his refrigerator and had his largest suitcase packed when he heard the buzzer for the outer door of the building. He hit the release to let Nolan in and waited there for him to come out of the elevator. "Hey, man. Thanks for coming by."

Nolan smiled and straightened his tie as he walked down the hallway. It was the middle of the week, so he was dressed more for work than Heath, who was in his jeans and NYU alumni sweatshirt.

"How's your dad doing?" Nolan asked.

Heath urged him inside and shut the door. "He's stable. I think he's going to pull through fine, but as I mentioned earlier, I'm going to be gone a few months while he recovers."

"Totally understandable. I think everything will go smoothly at the office. The only account I worry about with you gone is J'Adore."

Heath went to the refrigerator and pulled out two bottles of sparkling water. He opened them both and handed one over to Nolan. "The cosmetics account? Why do they worry you?"

"Well—" Nolan shrugged "—it has more to do with the owner's preference for *Monsieur Langston*."

"Oh," Heath replied. Now he understood. The French cosmetics company was a great account. They'd helped J'Adore break into the high-end American cosmetics market in the last year. Thanks to his company's marketing campaign, J'Adore was the trendiest new product line for the wealthy elite. The only issue was the owner, Madame Cecilia Badeau. She was in her late fifties, wealthy and eccentric, and she had Heath in her sights. For a while he was concerned they would lose the account if he didn't make himself...*available* to her.

"Thank goodness you're married, man," Nolan said, flopping down onto the sleek, white leather couch.

There was that. It was the first time he was thankful to have that stupid piece of paper legally binding him to Julianne. In order not to offend Madame Badeau, Heath had to tell her he was married. It came as quite a shock to her, as well as Nolan, who was also in the room at the time. They were the only other people who knew he and Julianne were married. He explained that Julianne traveled for her work and was always out of town when he was asked about her. Madame Badeau had immediately backed off, but she still insisted the account be personally handled by Heath.

"I think she'll understand that I've taken a leave of absence."

Nolan looked at him, his dark brows pointedly drawn together with incredulity. "I sincerely hope so, but don't be surprised if you get a call."

"After a month on the farm, I might be happy to answer." Heath hadn't spent more than a few days back at the Garden of Eden Christmas Tree Farm since he'd graduated from college. Avoiding Julianne had meant avoiding his family, although he was beginning to think that was the wrong tactic. He was out of sight, out of mind with her. From now on, he was going to be up close and personal.

"Are you going to be running that huge place all by yourself?" Nolan asked.

"No," Heath said, sliding onto the other end of the couch. "Julianne is going back for a while, too."

Nolan sputtered, obviously trying not to choke on his sip of water. "Julianne? Your *wife*, Julianne?"

Heath sighed. "Technically, yes, but I assure you it means nothing. I mean, I told you we never even slept together, right?"

"I still don't know what you could've done to ruin a marriage within hours of your vows."

Heath had wondered that same thing a million times. One moment, he had achieved his life's dream and married his glorious Julianne. The next, she was hysterically crying and screaming for him to stop touching her. The moment he let her go, she ran into the bathroom of their hotel room and didn't come out for two hours.

"I don't know. She never would tell me what changed. She was happy. The perfect, beautiful blushing bride. She responded to me, physically. Things were going fine until they weren't. All she would ever say was that she was sorry. She thought she could be with me, but she just couldn't do it."

"Was she a virgin? My high-school girlfriend was a nervous wreck our first time."

"That's what I thought. I never asked her directly, that felt weird, but that was my assumption. I kept thinking she'd warm up to the idea. She didn't." When he'd first told his partner about his crazy marriage, Heath hadn't elaborated and Nolan had been kind enough not to press him for details. Now, facing months with Julianne, he was glad he had someone to talk to about it.

Nolan scoffed. "What about when you got home?"

"I was trying not to push her. She asked not to tell anyone about the marriage right away and I agreed. I thought she needed time, and we had a few weeks before we both went to school. One morning, I came in from the fields and her car was gone. She'd left early to go to Chicago and didn't tell me or say goodbye."

"What did you do?"

"I followed her up there. She wouldn't even let me into her room. I'd never seen such a hard, cold expression on her face before that day. She told me getting married was a mistake. She was so embarrassed, she couldn't bear to tell anyone about it. Then she told me to go home and forget it ever happened."

"Do you think there's more to it than what she told you?"

"Some days, yes, some days, no. I do think she was ashamed to tell people that she married me. Especially our parents. She's always been too concerned with what people think. Jules had to have Molly and Ken's approval for everything. Maybe she didn't think she would get it for our marriage."

"Or?"

That was the big question. Something just didn't add up. If she had been so concerned about their parents finding out what happened, she either wouldn't have married him at all or she would have panicked when they returned home and had to face telling them. But she had panicked on their wedding night without any warning that his eighteen-year-old self could pick up on. They had kissed and indulged in some fondling in the days before the wedding and again that night. It wasn't until all the clothes came off that the mood shifted.

Then there was fear in her eyes. Sudden terror. And he'd barely touched her, much less hurt her. He'd had eleven years to live that night over and over in his mind and still didn't know what he did wrong.

"I have no idea. I just know that whatever the issue is, she doesn't want to talk about it."

"Why are you two still married, then? You're not still in love with her, are you, Heath?"

"I'm not," Heath assured him. "That boyhood crush died a long time ago, but it's more complicated than that."

"Enlighten me."

"At first, I thought she would change her mind. We had broken up, but I was certain she would realize she was overreacting about the sex and after being apart for a while she would miss me and decide she really did love me and want to be with me." He sighed, remembering how many nights he'd lain in bed naively fantasizing about her revelation. "But she didn't. She just pretended it never happened and expected me to do the same. She wouldn't talk about it."

"Then divorce her," Nolan suggested. "Be done with it."

Heath shook his head. "I know that I should, but there's no way I'm letting her off the hook that easily. I definitely think it's time to wrap the whole thing up between us, but she left me. I'm going to make her finish the job."

Nolan didn't look convinced. "That hasn't worked so well for you so far."

"I just think she needs a little incentive. Something to push her to make a move."

"What have you got in mind?" Nolan asked, his eyes

lighting up with his wicked imagination. He was the perfect business partner for Heath. They were both devious to a fault, but Heath had the creativity and Nolan had the business smarts.

He could still picture her flushed cheeks and stuttering speech when she was faced with his half-naked body. That really was the key. "I'm going to go back to the house and help Jules set up her new studio there. I'll do everything I need to around the farm. But I'm not going to pretend like nothing ever happened between us. I'm not going to sit on my hands and ignore that we're still attracted to one another."

"You're still into her? After everything that has happened? That's kinda twisted, man."

Heath shrugged. "I can't help it. She's even more beautiful than she was back then. I've always been attracted to her, and if she was honest with herself, she'd have to admit she's still got a thing for me, too. I'm going to try to use it to my advantage. Sex was always our problem, so I intend to push the issue and make her so uncomfortable, she will be all too happy to file for divorce and put this behind her. By the time I come back to New York, I expect to be a free man."

Nolan nodded slowly and put his bottle of water onto the coffee table. "And that's what you want, right?"

Heath wasn't sure what his business partner meant by that. Of course he wanted this to be over. And it would be. There was no way that Julianne would take him up on his sexual advances. She'd run, just like she always did, and he could finally move on. Just because he was still attracted to Julianne didn't mean that anything would come of it.

"Absolutely." Heath smiled wide, thinking of all the ways he could torture his bride over the next few weeks.

When it was all said and done, he would get his divorce and they would finally be able to move on.

But he sure as hell wasn't going to make it easy on her.

No one was around when Julianne arrived in her small moving truck. She wouldn't admit it, but Heath had been right. She needed help moving. There was more than she could fit in the car, so she decided to skip the storage rental and just bring it all with her. By the time she had that realization, she was already in Sag Harbor staring down the piles of stuff she didn't remember accumulating, so she ended up renting a truck one-way and towing her Camaro behind it the whole way.

She pulled the truck up behind the bunkhouse, where it would be out of the way until she could unload everything. Her clothes and personal things could go into her bedroom, but all the supplies for her studio would have to wait. She'd scoped out the storage room before she left and knew it would take time to clean it out. She'd considered doing it then, but Heath had insisted she wait until he was back from New York and could help her.

She opened the door to the storage room to give it a second look. The room was dim, with only the light coming in from one window, so she felt around until she found a light switch. A couple of fluorescent bulbs kicked on, highlighting the dusty shelves and cardboard boxes that filled the space. Molly was right—with a little elbow grease it would be the perfect place for her to work.

The hardwood floors continued into the storage room. There were several sturdy shelving units and open spaces for her to put her equipment. The brand-new, top-of-the-line kiln she ordered would fit nicely into the corner. She couldn't wait to get settled in.

Julianne grabbed her large rolling suitcase and threw

a duffel bag over her shoulder. She hauled them slowly up the stairs and paused at the landing between the two bedrooms. She wasn't sure which one to use. She'd never slept in the bunkhouse before. Whenever she came home, she used her old room, but that was going to be unavailable for a few weeks at least until Dad was able to climb the stairs again. She reached for the doorknob on the left, pushing the door open with a loud creak.

It was a nice, big space. When she was younger the rooms had been equipped with bunk beds that would allow the Edens to take in up to eight foster children at a time. Wade, Brody, Xander and Heath had stayed at the Garden of Eden until they were grown, but there were a dozen other boys who came and went for short periods of time while their home situations straightened out.

She was relieved to see the old bunks had been replaced with two queen-sized beds. They had matching comforters and a nightstand between them. A large dresser flanked the opposite wall. She took a step in and noticed the closet door was ajar and a suitcase was lying open inside it. And a light was coming from under the bathroom door. Heath was back. She hadn't noticed his car.

Before she could turn around, the bathroom door opened and Heath stepped out. He was fresh from the shower. His hair was damp and combed back, his face pink and smooth from a hot shave. The broad, muscular chest she caught a glimpse of a few days before was just as impressive now, with its etched muscles and dark hair, only this time his skin was slick. He had a towel wrapped around his waist, thank goodness, but that was the only thing between her and a fully naked Heath.

Once upon a time, the sight of her naked husband had launched her into a complete panic attack. The cloud of confused emotions and fear had doused any arousal she might have felt. Eleven years and a lot of therapy later, only the dull ache of need was left when she looked at him.

Heath wasn't startled by her appearance. In fact, her appraising glance seemed to embolden him. He arched an eyebrow at her and then smiled the way he always seemed to when she was uncomfortable. "We've really got to stop meeting like this."

A flush rushed to her cheeks from a mix of embarrassment and instant arousal. She knew Heath could see it, so that just made the deep red color even worse. "I'm sorry. I've done it again." Julianne backed toward the door, averting her eyes to look at anything but his hard, wet body and mocking grin. "I parked the moving truck out back and didn't realize you were here. I was trying to figure out which room I should use."

"You're welcome to use this one," Heath said. He sat down on the edge of one of the beds and gave it a good test bounce. "That would prove interesting."

"Uh, no," she said, slipping back through the doorway. "The other room will be just fine."

Her hands were shaking as she gripped the handle of her luggage and rolled it to the opposite bedroom. When she opened the door, she found it to be exactly the same as the other one, only better, because it didn't have her cocky, naked husband in it.

She busied herself hanging up clothes in the closet and storing underthings in the dresser. Putting things away was a good distraction from the sexual thoughts and raging desire pumping through her veins.

Julianne was setting out the last of her toiletries in the bathroom when she turned and found Heath in her doorway, fully clothed.

"Do you need help bringing more things in?"

"Not tonight. Tomorrow, maybe we can work on clearing out the storage room and then I can unload the rest of my supplies there. There's no sense piling up things in the living room. I don't have to return the truck for a few days."

"Okay, good," he said, but he didn't leave.

Julianne stood, waiting for him to speak or do something, but he just leaned against her door frame. His hazel gaze studied her, his eyes narrowing in thought. A smile curled his lips. She had no idea what he was actually thinking, but it was unnerving to be scrutinized so closely.

Finally, she returned to putting her things away and tried to pretend he wasn't inspecting her every move. There was something about the way he watched her that made her very aware of her own body. It happened every time. He didn't have to say a word, yet she would feel the prickle of awareness start up the back of her neck. Her heart would begin pounding harder in her chest. The sound of her breath moving rapidly in and out of her lungs would become deafening.

Then came the heat. What would start as a warmness in her cheeks would spread through her whole body. Beads of perspiration would start to form at the nape of her neck and the valley between her breasts. Deep in her belly, a churning heat would grow warmer and warmer.

All with just a look. She tried desperately to ignore him because she knew how quickly these symptoms would devolve to blatant wanting, especially if he touched her. Eleven years ago, she was too frightened to do anything about her feelings, but she'd come a long way. There was nothing holding her back now. Whether or not Heath still wanted her, he seemed happy to push the issue. How the hell would she make it through the next few months with him so close by? With no brothers or other family here to distract them?

"I'm surprised you're staying in the bunkhouse," Heath said at last.

"Why is that?" Julianne didn't turn to look at him. Instead, she stuffed her empty duffel bag into her luggage and zipped it closed.

"I would've thought you'd want to stay as far away from me as possible. Then again," he added, "this might be your chance to indulge your secret desires without anyone finding out. Maybe you're finally ready to finish what we started."

Julianne turned to look at him with her hands planted on her hips. Hopefully her indignant attitude would mask how close to the truth he actually was. "Indulge my secret desires? Really, Heath?"

He shoved his hands into the pockets of his gray trousers and took a few slow, casual steps into the room. "Why else would you stay out here? I'm sure things in the big house are much nicer."

"They are," she replied matter-of-factly. "But Daddy will be coming home soon and there won't be a room for me there. Besides, being out here makes me feel more independent. My studio will be downstairs, so it's convenient and I'll be less likely to disturb Mom and Dad."

"Yes," he agreed. "You can stay up late and make all the noise you want. You could scream the walls down if you felt inclined."

Julianne clenched her hands into fists at her sides. "Stop making everything I say into a sexual innuendo. Yes, I will be staying out here with you, but that's only because it's the only place to go. If there were an alternative, I'd gladly take it."

Heath chuckled, but she could tell by the look on his face that he didn't believe a word she said. "You're an awfully arrogant bastard," she noted. "I do not want to sleep with you, Heath."

"You say that," he said, moving a few feet closer. "But I know you better than you'd like to think, Jules. I recognize that look in your eye. The color rushing to your cheeks. The rapid rise and fall of your breasts as you breathe harder. You're trying to convince yourself that you don't want me, but we both know that you hate leaving things unfinished. And you and I are most certainly unfinished."

He was right. Julianne was normally focused on every detail, be it in art or life. She was an overachiever. The only thing she'd found she couldn't manage was being a wife. Just another reason to keep their past relationship under the covers.

A tingle of desire ran down her spine and she closed her eyes tightly to block it out. Wrong choice of words.

"Were you this arrogant when we eloped?" she asked. "I can't fathom that I would've fallen for you with an ego this large."

Heath looked at her, the smile curling his lips fading until a hard, straight line appeared across his face. "No, I wasn't this arrogant. I was young and naive and hopelessly in love with a girl that I thought cared about me."

"Heath, I—"

"Don't," he interrupted. He took another step forward, forcing Julianne to move back until the knobs of the dresser pressed into her rear end. "Don't say what you were going to say because you and I both know it's a waste of breath. Don't tell me that you were confused and scared about your feelings for me, because you knew exactly what you were doing. Don't bother to tell me it was just a youthful mistake, because it's a mistake that you refuse to correct. Why is that, I wonder?"

Julianne stood, trapped between her dresser and Heath's

looming body. He leaned into her and was so close that if she let out the breath she was holding and her muscles relaxed, they might touch. Unable to escape, her eyes went to the sensual curve of his mouth. She didn't care for what he was saying, but she would enjoy watching him say it. He had a beautiful mouth, one that she'd secretly fantasized about kissing long before they'd gone to Europe and long after they came back.

"Maybe," he added, "it's because you aren't ready to let go of me just yet."

It was just complicated. She'd wrestled with this for years. She wanted Heath, but the price of having him was too high for both of them to pay. And yet giving up would mean letting go of the best thing that ever happened to her. "Heath, I—"

"You can lie to everyone else," he interrupted. "You can even lie to yourself. But you can't lie to me, Jules. For whatever reason, the time wasn't right back then. Maybe we were just too young, but that's no longer the case. You want me. I want you. It's not right or wrong, black or white. It's just a fact."

His lips were a whisper away from hers. Her own mouth was suddenly dry as he spoke such blunt words with such a seductive voice. She couldn't answer him. She could barely think with him this close to her. Every breath was thick with the warm scent of his cologne and the soap from his shower.

Heath brought his hand up to caress her cheek. "It's time for you to figure out what you're going to do about it."

Julianne's brow drew down into a frown. "What I'm going to do about it?"

"Yes. It's pretty simple, Jules. You either admit that you want me and give yourself freely and enthusiastically to your husband at last. Or…you get off your hind end and file for divorce."

Julianne's mind went to the last discussion she'd had with her attorney. He could draw up the paperwork anytime. It was a pretty cut-and-dried arrangement with no comingled assets. She just had to tell him to pull the trigger. It was that simple and yet the thought made her nearly sick to her stomach. But what was her alternative? Staying married wouldn't solve their problems. And if marriage meant sleeping with Heath, there would just be sex clouding their issues.

"Why can't this wait until we're both back in New York and can work through the paperwork privately? Don't we have enough going on right now? I'm not really interested in either of your options."

A wicked grin curled Heath's full lips, making her heart stutter in her chest. "Oh, you will be. There's no more stalling, Jules. We've both lived in New York long enough to have addressed it privately, if that was what you really wanted. If you don't choose, I'll make the decision for you. And if *I* file for divorce, I'll go to Frank Hartman."

Frank Hartman was the family attorney and the only one in Cornwall. Even if Heath didn't spread the news she had no doubt that their parents would find out about their marriage if he filed with him. That would raise too many questions.

"Your dirty little secret will be out in the open for sure. I'll see to it that every single person in town finds out about our divorce." His lips barely grazed hers as he spoke, and then he started to laugh. He took a large step back, finally allowing her a supply of her very own oxygen.

"You think on that," he said, turning and walking out of her bedroom.

Four

Heath stumbled downstairs the next morning after pulling on some clothes. He could smell coffee and although still half-asleep, he was on a mission for caffeine. He'd slept late that morning after lying in bed for hours thinking about Julianne. After he'd walked out of her room, he'd shut his door, hoping to keep thoughts of her on the other side. He'd failed.

It would take a hell of a lot more than a panel of wood to do that. Not after being so close to her after all this time apart. Not after seeing her react to him. She was stubborn, he knew that, but she'd gotten under his skin just as he'd gotten under hers.

Part of him had enjoyed torturing her a little bit. He wasn't a vindictive person, but she did owe him a little after what she'd done. He wasn't going to get a wife or an apology out of all this. He'd just be a lonely divorced guy who couldn't tell the people he was closest to that he was a lonely divorced guy. His brothers, whom he typically turned to for advice or commiseration, couldn't know the truth. Poor Nolan would end up with the burden of his drama. He could at least watch her squirm a little bit and get some satisfaction from that. The whole point was to make her so uncomfortable that she would contact her lawyer.

But what had bothered him the most, what had kept him up until two in the morning, had been the look in her eyes when he'd nearly kissed her. He'd been close enough. Just the slightest move and their mouths would have touched. And she wanted him to kiss her. She'd licked her lips, her gaze focused on his mouth with an intensity like never before. It made him wonder what she would have done if he had.

He hadn't kissed Julianne since their wedding night. Heath never imagined that would be the last time he would kiss his wife. They'd been married literally a few hours. Certainly things wouldn't go bad that quickly. Right?

With a groan, he crossed the room, his gaze zeroing in on the coffeepot, half the carafe still full. He poured himself a cup and turned just in time to see Julianne shuffle into the kitchen with a giant cardboard box in her arms.

Despite the chilly October weather outside, she had already worked up a sweat moving boxes. She was wearing a thin tank top and a pair of cutoff jean shorts. Her long blond hair was pulled up into a messy bun on the top of her head with damp strands plastered to the back of her neck.

Heath forced down a large sip of hot coffee to keep from sputtering it everywhere. Man, she had an amazing figure. The girl he'd married had been just that—a girl. She'd been a tomboy and a bit of a late bloomer. She had still been fairly thin, a tiny pixie of a thing that he sometimes worried he might snap when he finally made love to her.

Things had certainly changed since the last time he'd run his hands over that body. He'd heard her complain to Molly about how she'd gained weight over the years, but he didn't mind. The tight little shorts she was wearing were filled out nicely and her top left little to his imagination. His brain might not be fully awake yet, but the rest of his body was up and at 'em.

"What?"

Julianne's voice jerked him out of his detailed assessment. He was staring and she'd caught him. Only fair after her heavy appraisal of him over the last few days. "You're going to hurt yourself," Heath quickly noted. He tried leaning casually against the kitchen counter to cover the tension in his body.

Her cool green gaze regarded him a moment before she dropped the box by the staircase with a loud thud and a cloud of dust. It joined a pile of four or five other equally dusty boxes. "I'm supposed to be helping you with that," he added when she didn't respond.

She turned back to him, rubbing her dirty palms on her round, denim-clad rear end. "I couldn't sleep," she said, disappearing into the storage room. A moment later she came back out with another box. "You weren't awake."

"I'm awake now."

She dropped the box to the floor with the others. "Good. You can start helping anytime then." Julianne returned to her chores.

"Good morning to you, too," he grumbled, drinking the last of his coffee in one large sip. Heath put his mug in the sink and walked across the room to join her in the storage room.

He looked around the space, surveying the work ahead of them. Clearing out the room would be less work than figuring out what to do with all the stuff. He plucked an old, flattened basketball out of one box and smashed it between his hands. Just one of a hundred unwanted things left behind over the years. They'd probably need to run a couple loads to the dump in Ken's truck.

"Is there a plan?" he asked.

Julianne rubbed her forearm across her brow to wipe away perspiration. "I'd like to clear the room out first. Then clean it so we can move my things in and I can return the truck. Then we can deal with the stuff we've taken out."

"Fair enough." Heath tossed the ball back into the box and picked it up.

They worked together quietly for the next hour or so. After the previous night's declarations, he expected her to say something, but he'd underestimated Julianne's ability to compartmentalize things. Today's task was cleaning the storeroom, so that was her focus. She'd used the same trick to ignore their relationship for other pursuits over the years. He didn't push the issue. They'd get a lot less cleaning done if they were arguing.

When the room was finally empty, they attacked the space with brooms and old rags, dusting away the cobwebs and sweeping up years of dust and grime. Despite their dirty chores, he couldn't help but stop and watch Julianne every now and then. She would occasionally bend over for something, giving him a prime view of her firm thighs and round behind. The sweat dampened her shirt and he would periodically catch a glimpse as a bead of perspiration traveled down into the valley between her breasts.

He wasn't sure if it was the hard work or the view, but it didn't take long for Heath to get overheated. As they were cleaning the empty room, he had to whip his shirt off and toss it onto the kitchen table. He returned to working, paying no attention to what was going on until he noticed Julianne was watching him and not moving any longer.

Heath paused and looked up at her. She had her arms crossed over her chest, suggestively pressing her small, firm breasts together. He might enjoy the view if not for the irritated expression puckering her delicate brow. "Is something wrong, Jules?"

"Do you normally run around half-naked or is all this just a show for my benefit?"

"What?" Heath looked down at his bare chest and tried to determine what was so offensive about it. "No, of course I don't run around naked. But I'm also not usually doing hard, dirty labor. Advertising doesn't work up much of a sweat."

Julianne was frowning, but he could see the slight twist of amusement in her lips. He could tell she liked what she saw, even if she wouldn't admit that to herself.

"It seems like every time I turn around, you're not wearing a shirt."

Heath smiled. "Is that a complaint or a pleasant observation?"

Julianne planted her hands on her hips, answering him without speaking.

"Well, to be fair, *you've* barged into my bedroom twice and caught me in various states of undress. That's not my fault. That's like complaining because I don't wear clothes into the shower. You make it sound like I've paraded around like a Chippendales dancer or something." Heath held out his arms, flexing his muscles and gyrating his hips for effect.

Julianne brought her hand to her mouth to stifle a giggle as he danced. "Stop that!" she finally yelled, throwing her dust rag at him.

Heath caught it and ended his performance. "You're just lucky I left my tear-away pants in Manhattan."

She shook her head with a reluctant smile and turned

back to what she'd been cleaning. They finished not too long after that, then piled their brooms and mops in the kitchen and went back in to look around.

"This isn't a bad space at all," Julianne said as they surveyed the empty, clean room. "I think it will make the perfect studio."

Heath watched her walk around the space, thinking aloud. "Is it big enough for all of your things?"

"I think so. If I put the new kiln over here," she said, "my big table will fit here. I can use this shelf to put my pieces on that are in progress. My pottery wheel can go here." She gestured to a space below the window. "And this old dresser will be good to store tools and supplies."

She seemed to have it all laid out in her mind. They just had to bring everything in. "Are you ready to unload the truck?"

Julianne shook her head and smoothed her palm over the wild strands of her hair. "Maybe later this afternoon. I'm exhausted. Right now, all I want to do is take a shower and get some lunch."

Heath couldn't agree more. "I'll probably do the same. But proceed with caution," he said.

"Caution?" Julianne looked at him with wide, concerned eyes.

"Yes. I *will* be naked up there. And wet," he added with a sly grin. "You've been forewarned."

Julianne was certain this was going to be the longest few months in history.

She'd quickly taken her shower and sat down on the edge of the bed to dry her hair. She could hear the water running in his bathroom when she was finished, making her think of his warning. He was wet and naked in the next room. She was determined to miss out on that event this time. Running into him once was an accident. Twice could be considered a fluke. A third time was stalking. Julianne wasn't about to give Heath the satisfaction of knowing she enjoyed looking at him. She did; he had a beautiful body. But she'd already gotten her daily eyeful of his hot, sweaty muscles as they worked downstairs.

That was more than enough to fire up her suppressed libido and set her mind to thinking about anything but cleaning. She shouldn't feel this way. It had been over a month since Danny moved out. Not a tragic dry spell by any means and she was more than capable of managing her urges. But somehow, the combination of Heath's friendly eyes, charming smile and hard body made her forget about all that.

It had been like that back in high school. She had gone years having Heath live with her family, trying to keep her attraction to him in check. Heath had been the first boy she'd ever kissed. She liked him. But somehow, once he came to the farm, it seemed inappropriate. So she tried to ignore it as he got older and grew more handsome. She tried to tell herself they were just friends when they would talk for hours.

By their senior year, they were the only kids left on the farm and it was getting harder for her to ignore the sizzle of tension between them. After what had happened to her five years earlier, she hadn't really dated. She'd kissed a boy or two, but nothing serious and nothing remotely close enough to hit her panic button. It was easy. Heath was the only one who got her blood pumping. The one who made her whole body tingle and ache to be touched. So she avoided him.

But it wasn't until they were alone in Paris that she let herself indulge her attraction. There, with the romantic twinkling lights and soft music serenading them, he'd told her he loved her. That he'd always loved her. This had to be the right thing to do. She loved him. He was her best friend. Heath would never hurt her. It was perfect.

Until her nerves got the best of her. Kissing was great. Roaming hands were very nice. But anything more serious made her heart race unpleasantly. Heath thought maybe she was saving herself for marriage and that would remove the last of her doubts. So they got married. And it only got worse.

Julianne sighed and carried the blow-dryer back into the bathroom. Funny how the thing that was supposed to bring them together forever—the ultimate relationship step—was what ended up dooming them.

It was easy to forget about her problems when her brushes with Heath were few and far between. They were both busy, and usually he didn't want to talk about their issues any more than she did. That did not seem to be the case any longer. She could tell that something had gotten into him, but she didn't know what. Perhaps Ken's second heart attack made him realize life was too short to waste it married to someone who didn't love him like she should. Or maybe he'd found someone else but hadn't told anyone about it yet.

That thought was enough to propel her out of the room and downstairs for some lunch. She didn't like thinking about Heath with someone else. That called for an edible distraction. It was a terrible habit to have, but she was an emotional eater. It had started after Tommy attacked her and it became a constant battle for her after that. Her therapist had helped her recognize the issue and to stop before she started, but when things weren't going well, it was nothing a cheeseburger and a Diet Coke wouldn't fix. At least for an hour or so.

At the top of the staircase, Julianne paused. She could

hear Heath's voice carrying from the kitchen. At first, Julianne thought he might be talking to her. She started down the stairs but stopped when she heard him speak again. He was on the phone.

"Hey, sweetheart."

Sweetheart? Julianne held her breath and took a step backward so he wouldn't see her on the stairs listening in. Who was he talking to? A dull ache in her stomach that had nothing to do with hunger told her she'd been right before. He hadn't mentioned dating anyone recently, but that must be what all the sudden divorce talk was about. Why would he tell her if he were seeing someone special? She was a slip of paper away from being his ex-wife, all things considered.

"Aww, I miss you, too." Heath listened for a moment before laughing. "I know it's hard, but I'll be back before you know it."

There was a tone to his voice that she wasn't used to hearing—an intimacy and softness she remembered from the time they spent together in Europe. This woman obviously had a special place in Heath's life. Julianne was immediately struck with a pang of jealousy as she listened in. It was stupid. They'd agreed that if they weren't together, they were both free to see other people. She'd been living with Danny for a year and a half, so she couldn't complain.

"You know I have to take care of some things here. But look on the bright side. When all this is handled and I come home, we can make that Caribbean vacation you've been dreaming about a reality. But you've got to be patient."

"Hang on, baby," Julianne muttered to herself with a mocking tone. "I gotta ditch the wife, then we can go frolic on the beach." And to think he'd been acting like he had been interested in something more between them. When he'd pressed against her, she was certain he still wanted her—at least short-term. He apparently had longer-term plans with someone else.

"Okay. I'll call again soon. 'Bye, darling."

Julianne choked down her irritation and descended the stairs with loud, stomping feet. When she turned toward the kitchen, Heath was leaning casually against the counter, holding his cell phone and looking pointedly at her. He had changed into a snug pair of designer jeans that hugged the thick muscles of his thighs and a button-down shirt in a mossy green that matched the color of his eyes. This was a middle-of-the-road look, a comfortable median between his sleepy casual style and his corporate shark suits. He looked handsome, put together and, judging by the light in his eyes, amused by her irritation.

"Something the matter?" he asked.

"No," she said quickly. There wasn't anything wrong. He could do whatever and whomever he wanted. That wasn't any concern of hers, no matter how spun up she seemed to be at the moment.

It was just because she'd never been faced with it before. That was it. Neither she nor Heath had ever brought anyone home to meet the family. They both dated, but it was an abstract concept that wasn't waved in her face like a red cape in front of a bull.

"I know you were listening in on my conversation."

She took a deep breath and shrugged. "Not really, but it was hard to ignore with all that mushy sweetheart nonsense."

The corners of Heath's mouth curled in amusement. "What's the matter, Jules? Are you jealous?"

"Why on earth would I be jealous?" she scoffed. "We're married, but it doesn't really mean anything. You're free to do what you want. I mean, if I wanted you, I could've had you, so obviously, I wouldn't be jealous."

"I don't know," Heath said, his brow furrowing. "Maybe you're starting to regret your decision."

"Not at all."

She said the words too quickly, too forcefully, and saw a flash of pain in Heath's light hazel eyes. It disappeared quickly, a smile covering his emotions the way it always did. Humor was his go-to defense mechanism. It could be maddening sometimes.

"You seem very confident in your decision considering you still haven't filed for divorce after all this time. Are you sure you want rid of me? Actions speak louder than words, Jules."

"Absolutely certain. I've just been too busy building my career to worry about something that seems so trivial after all this time."

Heath's jaw flexed as he considered her statement for a moment. He obviously didn't care for her choice of words. "We've never really talked about it. At least not without yelling. Since it's so *trivial*, care to finally tell me what went wrong? I've waited a long time to find out."

Julianne closed her eyes and sighed. She'd almost prefer his heated pursuit to the questions she couldn't answer. "I'd really rather not, Heath. What does it matter now?"

"You left me confused and embarrassed on my wedding night. Do you know how messed up it was to take my clothes off in front of a girl for the first time and have you react like that? It's ego-crushing, Jules. It may have been more than a decade ago, but it still matters."

Julianne planted her hands on her hips and looked down at the floor. This was no time for her to come clean. She couldn't. "I don't have anything more to tell you than I did before. I realized it was a mistake. I'm sorry I didn't correct it until that inopportune time."

Heath flinched and frowned at her direct words. "You seemed happy enough about it until then."

"We were in Europe. Everything was romantic and exciting and we were so far from home I could forget all the reasons why it was a bad idea. When faced with…" Her voice trailed off as she remembered the moment her panic hit her like a tidal wave. He was obviously self-conscious enough about her reaction. How could she ever explain to him that it wasn't the sight of his naked body per se, but the idea of what was to come that threw her into a flashback of the worst day of her life? She couldn't. It would only hurt him more to know the truth. "When faced with the point of no return, I knew I couldn't go through with it. I know you want some big, drawn-out explanation as though I'm holding something back, but I'm not. That's all there is to it."

"You are so full of crap. I've known you since we were nine years old. You're lying. I know you're lying. I just don't know what you're lying about." Heath stuck his hands in his pockets and took a few leisurely steps toward her. "But maybe I'm overthinking it. Maybe the truth of the matter is that you're just selfish."

He might as well have slapped her. "Selfish? I'm selfish?" That was great. She was lying to protect him. She'd left him so he could find someone who deserved his love, but somehow she was selfish.

"I think so. You want your cake and you want to eat it, too." Heath held out his arms. "It doesn't have to be that way. If you want me, I'm right here. Take a bite. Please," he added with emphasis, his gaze pinning her on the spot and daring her to reach out for him.

Julianne froze, not certain what to do or say. Part of her brain was urging her to leap into his arms and take what he had to give. She wasn't a scared teenager anymore. She could indulge and enjoy everything she couldn't have before. The other part worried about what it would lead to. Her divorce attorney's number was programmed into her phone. Why start something that they were on the verge of finishing for good?

"Maybe this will help you decide." Heath's hands went to her waist, pulling her body tight against him. Julianne stumbled a bit, colliding with his chest and placing her hands on his shoulders to catch herself. Her palms made contact with the hard wall of muscle she had seen so many times the last few days but didn't dare touch. The scent of his shower-fresh skin filled her nose. The assault on her senses made her head swim and her skin tingle with longing to keep exploring her newfound discovery.

She looked up at him in surprise, not quite sure what to do. His lips found hers before she could decide. At first, she was taken aback by the forceful claim of her mouth. This was no timid teenager kissing her. The hard, masculine wall pressed against her was all grown up.

In their youth, he had never handled her with less care than he would a fragile piece of pottery. Now, he had lost what control he had. And she liked it. They had more than a decade of pent-up sexual tension, frustration and downright anger between them. It poured out of his fingertips, and pressed into her soft flesh, drawing cries of pleasure mingled with pain in the back of her throat.

Matching his ferocity, she clung to his neck, pulling him closer until his body was awkwardly arched over hers. Every place he touched seemed to light on fire until her whole body burned for him. She was getting lost in him, just as she had back then.

And then he pulled away. She had to clutch at the countertop to stay upright once his hard body withdrew its support.

His hazel eyes raked over her body, noting her undeniable response to his kiss. "So what's it going to be, Jules? Are the two of us over and done? Decide."

There were no words. Her brain was still trying to process everything that just happened. Her body ached for him to touch her again. Her indecisiveness drew a disappointed frown across his face.

"Or," he continued, dropping his arms to his side, "do like you've always done. A big nothing. You say you don't want me, but you don't want anyone else to have me, either. You can't have it both ways. You've got to make up your mind, Jules. It's been eleven years. Either you want me or you don't."

"I don't think the two of us are a good idea," she admitted at last. That was true. They weren't a good idea. Her body just didn't care.

"Then what are you waiting for? End it before you sink your next relationship." Heath paused, his brow furrowing in thought. "Unless that's how you like it."

"How I like what?"

"Our marriage is your little barrier to the world. You've dated at least seven or eight guys that I know of, none of them ever getting serious. But that's the way you want it. As long as you're married, you don't have to take it to the next level."

"You think I like failing? You think I want to spend every Christmas here watching everyone snuggled up into happy little couples while I'm still alone?"

"I think a part of you does. It might suck to be alone, but it's better than making yourself vulnerable and getting hurt. Trust me, I know what it's like to get your heart ripped out and stomped on. Being lonely doesn't come close to that kind of pain. I'm tired of you using me, Jules. Make a decision."

"Fine!" Julianne pushed past him, her vision going red as she stomped upstairs into her room. He'd kissed her and insulted her in less than a minute's time. If he thought she secretly wanted to be with him, he was very, very wrong. She snatched her cell phone off the bed and went back to the kitchen.

By the time she returned, the phone was ringing at her attorney's office. "Hello? This is Julianne Eden." Her gaze burrowed into Heath's as she spoke. "Would you please let Mr. Winters know that I'm ready to go forward with the divorce paperwork? Yes. Please overnight it to my secondary address in Connecticut. Thank you."

She slammed her phone onto the kitchen table with a loud smack that echoed through the room. "If you want a divorce so damn bad, fine. Consider it done!"

Five

The rest of the afternoon and most of the next day were spent working. They focused on their chores, neither willing to broach the subject of their argument and set off another battle. The divorce papers would arrive at any time. They had things to get done. There was no sense rehashing it.

They were unloading the last of her equipment from the rental truck when Heath spied Sheriff Duke's patrol car coming up the driveway.

Julianne was beside him, frozen like a deer in the oncoming lights of a car. He handed her the box he'd been carrying. "Take this and go inside. Don't come out unless I come get you."

She didn't argue. She took the box and disappeared through the back door of the storage room. He shut the door behind her and walked around the bunkhouse to where Duke's Crown Victoria was parked beside his Porsche.

Duke climbed out, eyeballing the sports car as he rounded it to where Heath was standing. "Afternoon, Heath."

Heath shook his hand politely and then crossed his arms over his chest. This wasn't a social call and he wouldn't let his guard down for even a second thinking that it was. "Evening, Sheriff. What can I do for you?"

Duke slipped off his hat, gripping it in his left hand. "I just came from the hospital. I spoke with your folks."

Heath tried to keep the anger from leaching into his voice, but the tight clench of his jaw made his emotions obvious as he spoke. "You interviewed my father in the hospital after open-heart surgery? After he had a heart attack the last time you spoke? Did you try to arrest him this time, too?"

"He's not in critical condition," Duke said. "Relax. He's fine. Was when I got there and was when I left. The doctors say he's doing better than expected."

Heath took a deep breath and tried to uncoil his tense muscles. He still wasn't happy, but at least Ken was okay. "I assume you're not here to give me an update on Dad as a public service to the hospital."

A faint smile curled Duke's lips. "No, I'm not. Would you care to sit down somewhere?"

"Do I need a lawyer?" Heath asked.

"No. Just wanting to ask a few questions. You're not a suspect at this time."

"Then no, I'm fine standing." Heath wasn't interested in getting comfortable and drawing out this conversation. He could outstand the older officer by a long shot. "What can I help you with?"

Duke nodded softly, obviously realizing he wasn't going to be offered a seat and some tea like he would if Molly were home. "First, I wanted to let you know that Ken and

Molly are no longer suspects. I was finally able to verify their story with accounts of others in town."

"Like what?" Heath asked.

"Well, Ken had always maintained he was sick in bed all that day with the flu. I spoke to the family physician and had him pull old records from the archives. Ken did come in the day before to see the doctor. Doc said it was a particularly bad strain of flu that year. Most people were in bed for at least two days. I don't figure Ken was out in the woods burying a body in the shape he was in."

"He was sick," Heath added. "Very sick. Just as we've told you before."

"People tell me a lot of things, Heath. Doesn't make it true. I've got to corroborate it with other statements. We've established Ken was sick that day. So, how did that work on the farm? If Ken wasn't working, did the whole group take the day off?"

"No," Heath answered with a bit of a chuckle. Sheriff Duke obviously hadn't grown up on a farm. "Life doesn't just stop when the boss is feeling poorly. We went on with our chores as usual. Wade picked up a few of the things that Ken normally did. Nothing particularly special about it. That's what we did whenever anyone was sick."

"And what about Tommy?"

"What about him?" Heath wasn't going to volunteer anything without being asked directly.

"What was he doing that day?"

Heath sighed and tried to think back. "It's been a long time, Sheriff, but if I had to guess, I'd figure he was doing a lot of nothing. That's what he did most days. He tended to go out into the trees and mess around. I never saw him put in an honest afternoon's work."

"I heard he got into some fights with the other boys."

Heath wasn't going to let Duke zero in on his brothers

as suspects. "That's because he was lazy and violent. He had a quick temper and, on more than one occasion, took it out on one of us."

Sheriff Duke's dark gaze flicked over Heath's face for a moment as he considered his answers. "I bet you didn't care much for Tommy."

"No one did. You know what kind of stuff he was into."

"I can't comment on that. You know his juvenile files are sealed."

"I don't need to see his files to know what he'd done. I lived with him. I've got a scar from where he shoved me into a bookcase and split my eyebrow open. I remember Wade's black eye. I know about the stealing and the drugs and the fights at school. You can't seal my memories, Sheriff." Some days he wished he could.

Duke shuffled uncomfortably on his feet. "When was the last time you saw Tommy?"

"The last time I saw him…" Heath tried to remember back to that day. He spent most of his time trying not to think about it. The image of Tommy's blank, dead stare and the pool of blood soaking into the dirt was the first thing to come to mind. He quickly put that thought away and backed up to before that moment. Before he heard the screams and found Tommy and Julianne together on the ground. "It was just after school. We all came home, Molly brought us some snacks to the bunkhouse and told us Ken was sick in bed. We finished up and each headed out to do our chores. I went into the eastern fields."

"Did you see Tommy go into the woods that day?"

"No." And he hadn't. "Tommy was still sitting at the kitchen table when I left. But that's where he should've been going."

"Was he acting strangely that day?"

He had been. "He was a little quieter than usual. More

withdrawn. I figured he'd had a bad day at school." Tommy had also been silently eyeing Julianne with an interest he didn't care for. But he wasn't going to tell Duke that. No matter what happened between the two of them and their marriage, that wouldn't change. He'd sworn to keep that secret, to protect her above all else, and he would. Even if he grew to despise her one day, he would keep his promise.

"Had he ever mentioned leaving?"

"Every day," Heath said, and that was true. "He was always talking big about how he couldn't wait to get away. He said we were like some stupid television sitcom family and he couldn't stand any of us. He said that when he was eighteen, he was getting the hell out of this place. Tommy didn't even care about finishing school. I suppose a diploma didn't factor much into the lines of work he was drawn to. When he disappeared that day, I always figured he decided not to wait. His birthday was coming up."

Duke had finally taken out a notepad and was writing a few things down. "What made you think he ran away?"

This was the point at which he had to very carefully dance around the truth. "Well, Wade found a note on his bed. And his stuff wasn't in his room when we looked the next morning." The note and the missing belongings were well-documented from the original missing-persons report. The fact that they never compared the handwriting to any of the other children on the farm wasn't Heath's fault. "It all added up for me. With Ken sick, it might have seemed like the right day to make his move." Unfortunately, he'd made his move on Julianne when she was alone in the trees.

"Did he ever talk to you about anything? His friends or his plans?"

At that, a nervous bit of laughter escaped Heath's lips. "I was a scrawny, thirteen-year-old twerp that did nothing but get in his way. Tommy didn't confide in anyone, but especially not in me."

"He didn't talk to your brothers?"

Heath shrugged. "Tommy shared a room with Wade. Maybe he talked to him there. But he was never much for chatting with the rest of us. More than anything he talked *at* us, not *to* us. He said nothing but ugly things to Brody, so he avoided Tommy. Xander always liked to keep friendly with everyone, but even he kept his distance."

"And what about Julianne?"

Heath swallowed hard. It was the first time her name had been spoken aloud in the conversation and he didn't like it. "What about her?"

"Did she have much to do with Tommy?"

"No," Heath said a touch too forcefully. Sheriff Duke looked up at him curiously. "I mean, there was no reason to. She lived in the big house and still went to junior high with me. If they spoke, it was only in passing or out of politeness on her part."

Duke wrote down a few things. Heath wished what he'd said had been true. That Tommy hadn't given the slightest notice to the tiny blonde. But as much as Julianne tried to avoid him, Tommy always found a way to intersect her path. She knew he was dangerous. They all did. They just didn't know what to do about it.

"Were they ever alone together?"

At that, Heath slowly shook his head. He hoped the sheriff didn't see the regret in his eyes or hear it in his voice as he spoke. "Only a fool would have left a little girl alone with a predator like Tommy."

Heath had been quiet and withdrawn that night. Julianne expected him to say *something*. About what happened with Sheriff Duke, about their kiss, about their argument or the divorce papers...but nothing happened. After Duke left, Heath had returned to unloading the truck. When that was done, he volunteered to drive into town and pick up a pizza.

While he was gone, the courier arrived with the package from her attorney. She flipped through it, giving it a cursory examination, and then dropped it onto the kitchen table. She wasn't in the mood to deal with that today.

Heath's mood hadn't improved by the time he got back. He was seated on the couch, balancing his plate in his lap and eating almost mechanically. Julianne had opted to eat at the table, which gave her a decent view of both Heath and the television without crowding in his space.

There was one cold slice of pizza remaining when Julianne finally got the nerve to speak. "Heath?"

He looked startled, as though she'd yanked him from the deep thoughts he was lost in. "Yes?"

"Are you going to tell me what happened?"

"You mean with Sheriff Duke?"

"I guess. Is that what's bothering you?"

"Yes and no," he replied, giving her an answer and not at the same time.

Julianne got up and walked over to the couch. She flopped down onto the opposite end. "It's been a long week, Heath. I'm too tired to play games. What's wrong?"

"Aside from the divorce papers sitting on the kitchen table?" Heath watched her for a moment before sighing heavily and shaking his head. "Sheriff Duke just asked some questions. Nothing to worry about. In fact, he told me Ken and Molly are no longer suspects."

Julianne's brow went up in surprise. "And that's good, right?"

"Absolutely. The conversation was fine. It just made me think." He paused. "It reminded me how big of a failure I am."

It didn't matter what happened between them recently. The minute he needed her support she would give it. "You? A failure? What are you talking about?" Every one of her brothers was at the top of their field with millions in their accounts. None were failures by a long shot. "You're the CEO of your own successful advertising agency. You have a great apartment in Manhattan. You drive a Porsche! How is that a failure?"

A snort of derision passed his lips and he turned away to look at the television. "I'm good at convincing people to buy things they don't need. Something to be proud of, right? But I fail at the important stuff. When it matters, it seems like nothing I say or do makes any difference."

She didn't like the tone of his voice. It was almost defeated. Broken. Very much unlike him and yet she knew somehow she was responsible. "Like what?"

"Protecting you. Protecting my parents. Ken. Saving our marriage…"

Julianne frowned and held her hands up. "Wait a minute. First, how is a nine-year-old boy supposed to save his parents in a car crash that he almost died in, too? Or keep Dad from having another heart attack?"

"It was my fault we were on that road. I pestered my father until he agreed to take us for ice cream."

"Christ, Heath, that doesn't make it your fault."

"Maybe, but Dad's heart attack *was* my fault. The second one at least. If I'd come clean to the cops about what happened with Tommy, they wouldn't have come here questioning him."

He was being completely irrational about this. Heath had been internalizing more things than she realized. "And what about me? How have you failed to protect me? I'm sitting right here, perfectly fine."

"Talking with Sheriff Duke made me realize I should've

seen it coming. With Tommy. I should've known he was going to come for you. And I left you alone. When I think about how bad it could've been…" His voice trailed off. "I never should've left you alone with him."

"You didn't leave me alone *with* him. I was doing my chores just like you were, and he found me. And you can't see the future. I certainly don't expect you to be able to anticipate the moves of a monster like he was. There's no reason why you should have thought I would be anything but safe."

He looked up at her at last, his brow furrowed with concern for things he couldn't change now. "But I *did* know. I saw the way he was looking at you. I knew what he was thinking. My mistake was not realizing he was bold enough to make a move. What if you hadn't been able to fight him off? What if he had raped you?" He shook his head, his thoughts too heavy with the possibilities to see Julianne stiffen in her seat. "I wish he had just run away. That would've been better for everyone."

The pained expression was etched deeply into his forehead. He was so upset thinking Tommy had attacked her. She could never ever tell Heath how successful Tommy had been in getting what he'd wanted from her. He already carried too much of the blame on his own shoulders and without cause. Nothing that happened that day was his fault. "Not for the people he would have hurt later."

Heath shrugged away what might have been. "You give me credit for protecting you, but I didn't. If I had been smart, you wouldn't have needed protecting."

Julianne scooted closer to him on the couch and placed a comforting hand on his shoulder. "Heath, stop it. No one could have stopped Tommy. What's important is everything you did for me once it was done. You didn't have to do what you did. You've kept the truth from everyone all this time."

"Don't even say it out loud," he said with a warning tone. "I did what I had to do and no matter what happens with Sheriff Duke, I don't regret it. It was bad enough that you would always have memories of that day. I wasn't about to let you get in front of the whole town and have to relive it. That would be like letting him attack you over and over every time you had to tell the story."

It would have been awful, no question. No woman wants to stand up and describe being assaulted, much less a thirteen-year-old girl who barely understood what was happening to her. But she was strong. She liked to think that she could handle it. The boys had other ideas. They—Heath especially—thought the best thing to do was keep quiet. Unlike her, they had to live with the fear of being taken away. They made huge sacrifices for her, more than they even knew, and she was grateful. She just worried the price would end up being far higher than they intended to pay.

"But has it been worth the anxiety? The years of waiting for the other shoe to drop? We've been on pins and needles since Dad sold that property. If you had let me go to the police, it would be long over by now."

"See…" Heath said. "My attempt to protect you from the consequences of my previous failures failed as well. It made things worse in the long run. And you knew it, too. That's why you couldn't love me. You were embarrassed to be in love with me."

"What?" Julianne jerked her hand away in surprise. Where the hell had this come from?

Heath shifted in his seat to face her head-on. "Tell the truth, Jules. You might have been intimidated by having sex with me or what our future together might be, but the nail in the coffin was coming home and having to tell your parents that you'd married *me*. You were embarrassed."

"I was embarrassed, but not because of you. It was never about you. I was ashamed of how I'd let myself get so wrapped up in it that I didn't think things through. And then, what? How could we tell our parents that we eloped and broke up practically the same day?"

"You're always so worried about what other people think. Then and now. You'd put a stranger ahead of your own desires every time. Here you'd rather throw away everything we had together than disappoint Molly."

"We didn't have much to throw away, Heath. A week together is hardly a blip in the relationship radar." How many women had he dated for ten times as long and didn't even bother to mention it to the family? Like the woman on the phone packing her bags for the Caribbean?

"It makes a bigger impact when you're married, I assure you. What you threw away was the potential. The future and what we could have had. That's what keeps me up at night, Jules."

It had kept her up nights, too. "And what if it hadn't worked out? If we'd divorced a couple years later? Maybe remarried and brought our new spouses home. How would those family holidays go after that? Unbelievably awkward."

"More awkward than stealing glances of your secret, estranged wife across the dinner table?"

"Heath…"

"I don't think you understand, Jules. You never did. Somehow in your mind, it was just a mistake that had to be covered up so no one would find out. It was an infatuation run awry for you, but it was more than that for me. I loved you. More than anything. I wish I hadn't. I spent years trying to convince myself it was just a crush.

It would have been a hell of a lot easier to deal with your rejection if it were."

"Rejection? Heath, I didn't reject you."

"Oh, really? How does it read in your mind, Jules? In mine, the girl I loved agreed to marry me and then bolted the moment I touched her. Whether you were embarrassed of me or the situation or how it might look…in the end, my wife rejected me and left me in her dust. You went off to art school without saying goodbye and just pretended like our marriage and our feelings for each other didn't matter anymore. That sounds like a textbook definition for rejection."

Julianne sat back in her seat, trying to absorb everything he'd said. He was right. It would have been kinder if she'd just told him she didn't have feelings for him. It would have been a lie, but it would have been gentler on him than what she did.

"Heath, I never meant for you to feel that way. I'm sorry if my actions made you feel unwanted or unloved. I was young and confused. I didn't know what to do or how to handle everything. I do love you and I would never deliberately hurt you."

He snickered and turned away. "You love me, but you're not *in love* with me, right?"

She was about to respond but realized that confirming what he said would be just as hurtful as telling him she didn't love him at all. In truth, neither was entirely accurate. Her feelings were all twisted where Heath was concerned. They always had been and she'd never successfully straightened them out.

"Go ahead and say it."

Julianne sighed. "It's more complicated than that, Heath. I do love you. But not in the same way I love Xander or Brody or Wade, so no, I can't say that. There are other feelings. There always have been. Things that I don't know how to…"

"You want me."

It was a statement, not a question. She raised her gaze to meet his light hazel eyes. The golden starbursts in the center blended into a beautiful mix of greens and browns. Heath's eyes were always so expressive. Even when he tried to hide his feelings with a joke or a smile, Julianne could look him in the eye and know the truth.

The expression now was a difficult one. There was an awkward pain there, but something else. An intensity that demanded an honest answer from her. He knew she wanted him. To tell him otherwise would be to lie to them both. She tore her eyes away, hiding beneath the fringe of her lashes as she stared down at her hands. "I shouldn't."

"Why not? I thought you weren't embarrassed of me," he challenged.

"I'm not. But we're getting a divorce. What good would giving in to our attraction do?"

She looked up in time to see the pain and worry vanish from his expression, replaced by a wicked grin. "It would do a helluva lot of good for me."

Julianne was hard-pressed not to fall for his charming smile and naughty tone. "I'm sure you'd be pleased at the time. So would I. But then what? Is that all it is? Just sex? Is it worth it for just sex? If not, are we dating?"

"Running off with me was very much out of character for you," he noted. "You can't just do something because it feels good and you want to. You have to rationalize everything to the point that the fun is stripped right out."

"I'm trying to be smart about this! Fun or not, you want us to get divorced. Why would I leap back into your bed with both feet?"

"I didn't say I wanted us to get divorced."

That wasn't true. He'd had her pressed against the dresser when he'd made his ultimatum. He'd demanded it yesterday. The papers were three feet away. "I distinctly recall you—"

"Saying you needed to make a choice. Be with me or don't. No more straddling the fence. If you don't want me, then fine. But if you do…by all means, have me. I'm happy to put off the divorce while we indulge in our marital rights."

Julianne frowned. "Do you even hear yourself? Put off our divorce so we can sleep together?"

"Why not? I think I deserve a belated wedding night. We've had all of the drama of marriage with none of the perks."

"You just want to catch up on eleven years of sex."

"Maybe." He leaned in closer, the gold fire in his eyes alight with mischief. "Do you blame me?"

The low, suggestive rumble of his voice so close made her heart stutter in her chest. "S-stop acting like you've lived as a monk this whole time. Even if you did, eleven years is a lot to catch up on. We do still have a farm to run and I have a gallery show to work on."

"I'm all for making the most of our time together here. Give it the old college try."

Julianne shook her head. "And again, Heath, what does that leave us with? I want you, you want me. I'm not about to leap into all this again without thinking it through."

"Then don't leap, Jules. Test the waters. Slip your toe in and see how it feels." He smiled, slinking even closer to her. "I hear the water is warm and inviting." His palm flattened on her denim-covered thigh.

The heat was instantaneous, spreading quickly through her veins until a flush rushed to her cheeks. She knew that all she had to do was say the word and he would do all the things to her she'd fantasized about for years. But she wasn't ready to cross the line. He was right. She did strip the spontaneity out of everything, but she very rarely made decisions that haunted her the way she had with him. She didn't want to misstep this time. She had too many regrets where Heath was concerned. If and when she gave herself to him, she wanted to be fully content with making the right choice.

"I'm sure it is." She reached down and picked up his hand, placing it back in his own lap. "But the water will be just as warm tomorrow."

Six

Julianne rolled over and looked at the clock on the dresser. It was just after two in the morning. That was her usual middle-of-the-night wake-up time. She'd gone to sleep without issue, as always, but bad dreams had jerked her awake about thirty minutes ago and she'd yet to fall back asleep.

She used to be a fairly sound sleeper, but she woke up nearly every night now. Pretty much since Tommy's body was unearthed last Christmas. As much as they had all tried to put that day out of their heads, there was no escaping it. Even if her day-to-day life was too busy to dwell on it, her subconscious had seven to eight hours a night to focus on the worries and fears in the back of her mind.

As much as he wanted to, Heath couldn't protect her forever. Julianne was fairly certain that before she left this farm, the full story would be out in the open. Whether she would be moving out of the bunkhouse and into the jailhouse remained to be seen. Sheriff Duke smelled a rat and he wouldn't rest until he uncovered the truth. The question was whether the truth would be enough for him. A self-defense or justifiable homicide verdict wouldn't give him the moment of glory he sought.

With a sigh, Julianne sat up in bed and brushed the messy strands of her hair out of her face. Tonight's dream had been a doozy, waking her in a cold sweat. She had several different variations of the dream, but this was the one that bothered her the most. She was running through the Christmas-tree fields. Row after row of pine trees flew past her, but she didn't dare turn around. She knew that if she did, Tommy would catch her. The moment his large, meaty hand clamped onto her shoulder, Julianne would shoot up in bed, a scream dying in the back of her throat as she woke and realized that Tommy was long dead.

You would think after having the same nightmares over and over, they wouldn't bother her anymore, but it wasn't true. It seemed to get worse every time. Most nights, she climbed out of bed and crept into her workshop. Something about the movement of the clay in her hands was soothing. She would create beauty and by the time she cleaned up, she could return to sleep without hesitation or nightmares.

For the last week, she'd had no therapeutic outlet to help her fall back asleep. Instead she'd had to tough it out, and she would eventually drift off again around dawn. But now she had a functioning workshop downstairs and could return to the hypnotizing whirl of her pottery wheel.

She slipped silently from the bed and stepped out into the hallway. The house was quiet and dark. She moved quickly down the stairs, using her cell phone for light until she reached the ground floor. There, she turned on the kitchen light. She poured herself a glass of water, plucked an oatmeal raisin cookie from the jar on the counter and headed toward her new studio.

The fluorescent lights flickered for a moment before turning on, flooding the room with an odd yellow-white glow. Heath had worked very hard to help her get everything in place. A few boxes remained to be put away, and her kiln wouldn't be delivered for another day or two, but the majority of her new workshop was ready to start work.

Julianne finished her cookie and set her drink on the dresser, out of the way. One of the boxes on the floor near her feet had bricks of ready-to-use clay. She reached in to grab a one-pound cube and carried it over to her wheel. A plate went down on the wheel, then the ball of soft, moist gray clay on top of it. She filled a bucket with water and put her smoothing sponge in it to soak.

Pulling up to the wheel, she turned it on and it started to spin. She plunged her hands into the bucket to wet them and then closed her slick palms over the ball of clay. Her gallery showing would be mostly sculpted figurines and other art pieces, but the bread and butter of her shop in the Hamptons was stoneware pieces for the home. Her glazed bowls, mugs, salt dishes and flower vases could be found in almost any home in the area.

When she woke up in the night, vases were her go-to item. Her sculptures required a great deal of concentration and a focused eye. At three in the morning, the creation of a vase or bowl on her spinning wheel was a soothing, automatic process. It was by no means a simple task, but she'd created so many over the years that it came to her as second nature.

Her fingers slipped and glided in the wet clay, molding it into a small doughnut shape, then slowly coaxing it taller. She added more water and reached inside. The press of her fingertips distorted the shape, making the base wider.

Cupping the outside again, she tapered in the top, creating the traditional curved flower-vase shape. She flared the top, forming the lip.

With the sponge, she ran along the various edges and surfaces, smoothing out the rough and distorted areas. Last, she used a metal tool to trim away the excess clay at the base and turned off the wheel.

She sat back with a happy sigh and admired her handiwork. When she first started sculpting, a piece like that would have taken her five tries. It would have collapsed on itself or been lopsided. She would press too hard and her thumb would puncture the side. Now, a perfect piece could be created in minutes. She wished everything in her life was that easy.

"I've never gotten to watch you work before."

Julianne leapt at the sound of Heath's voice. She turned around in her rolling chair, her heart pounding a thousand beats a minute in her chest. She brought a hand to her throat, stopping just short of coating herself in wet clay. "You shouldn't sneak up on a girl like that."

He smiled sheepishly from the doorway. "Sorry. At least I waited until you were done."

Heath was leaning against the door frame in an old NYU T-shirt and a pair of flannel plaid boxer shorts, and for that, she was thankful. She would lose her resolve to resist him if he came down in nothing but a pair of pajama pants. As it was, the lean muscles of his legs were pulling her gaze down the length of his body.

"Did I wake you?" she asked.

"I don't recall hearing you get up, but I woke up for some reason and realized I forgot to plug my phone into the charger. I left it in the kitchen accidentally." He took a few steps into the workshop. "I can't believe how quickly you did that. You're amazing."

Julianne stood up from her stool and took her metal spatula out of the drawer beside her. Uncomfortable with his praise, she lifted the metal plate and moved the wet vase over onto the shelf to dry. "It's nothing."

"Don't be modest," he argued. "You're very talented."

Julianne started the wheel spinning again and turned away to hide her blush. "Would you like to learn to make something?"

"Really?"

"Sure. Come here," she said. She eyed his large frame for a moment, trying to figure out the best way to do this. "Since I'm so short, it's probably easiest if you stand behind me and reach over. I can guide your hands better that way."

Heath rolled the stool out of the way and moved to her back. "Like this?"

"Yes." She glanced back at the position she had deliberately put them in and realized how stupid it was. Perhaps she would be smarter to talk him out of this. "You're going to get dirty. Is that okay?"

He chuckled softly at her ear, making a sizzle of awareness run along the sensitive line of her neck. "Oh, no, I'd better change. These are my good flannel boxers."

Julianne smiled at his sharp, sarcastic tone and turned back to the wheel. No getting out of this now. "Okay, first, dip your hands in the water. You have to keep them good and wet."

They both dipped their hands in the bucket of water, then she cupped his hands over the clay and covered them with her own. "Feel the pressure I apply to you and match it with your fingers to the clay."

They moved back and forth between the water and the clay. All the while, Julianne forced herself to focus on the vase and not the heat of Heath's body at her back.

The warm breath along her neck was so distracting. Her mind kept straying to how it would feel if he kissed her there. She wanted him to. And then she would realize their sculpture was starting to sag and she would return her attention to their project.

"This feels weird," Heath laughed, gliding over the gray mound. The slippery form began to take shape, their fingers sliding around together, slick and smooth. "And a little dirty, frankly."

"It does," she admitted. On more than one occasion, she'd lost herself in the erotic slip and slide of the material in her hands and the rhythmic purr of the wheel. That experience was amplified by having him so close. "But try to control yourself," she said with a nervous giggle to hide her own building arousal. "I don't want you having dirty thoughts every time you see my artwork."

Heath's hands suddenly slipped out from beneath hers and glided up her bare arms to clutch her elbows. The cool slide of his clay-covered hands along her skin was in stark contrast to the firm press of heat at her back. It was obvious that she was not the only one turned on by the situation.

"Actually, the artwork isn't what inspires me...."

A ragged breath escaped her lips, but she didn't dare move. She continued working the vase on her own now, her shaky hands creating a subpar product. But she didn't care. If she let go, she would touch Heath and she wasn't sure she would be able to stop.

Easing back, Heath brushed her hair over the other shoulder and, as though he could read her mind, pressed a searing kiss just below her ear. She tipped her neck to the side, giving better access to his hungry mouth. He kissed, nibbled and teased, sending one bolt of pleasure after the other down her spine.

She arched her back, pressing the curve of her rear

into the hard ridge of his desire. That elicited a growl that vibrated low against her throat. One hand moved to her waist, tugging her hips back even harder against him.

"Jules…" he whispered, sending a shudder of desire through her body and a wave of goose bumps across her bare flesh.

She finally abandoned the clay, letting it collapse on itself, and switched off the wheel before she covered his hands with her own. Their fingers slipped in and out between each other, his hands moving over her body. "Yes?" she panted.

"You said the waters would be just as warm tomorrow. It's tomorrow," he said, punctuating his point with a gentle bite at her earlobe.

That it was.

Julianne had been wearing a flimsy little pajama set when he walked in, but Heath was pretty sure it was ruined. The thin cotton camisole and matching shorts were sweet and sexy at the same time. The clothes reminded him of the girl he'd fantasized about in high school, and the curves beneath it reminded him of the ripe, juicy peach of a woman she was now.

He couldn't stop touching her, even though he knew his hands were covered in clay. Gray smears were drying up on her arms and her bare shoulders. The shape of his hand was printed on the cotton daisy pattern of her pajamas. A streak of gray ran along the edge of her cheek.

And he didn't care.

It was sexy as hell. Julianne was always so put together and mature. He loved seeing her dirty. He was so turned on watching her skilled hands shape and mold the clay. He wanted those hands on himself so badly, he had to bite his own lip to keep from interrupting her before she was finished. Even now he could taste the faint metallic flavor of his own blood on his tongue.

When Julianne finally turned in his arms to face him, he had to stop himself from telling her she was the most beautiful thing he'd ever seen in his life. Messy hair, dirty face and all. He'd already made the mistake of telling her too much before. It was a far cry from a declaration of love, but he intended to play this second chance much closer to the vest.

Julianne looked up at him, her light green eyes grazing over every inch of his face before she put her hands on each side of his head and tugged his mouth down to hers. The instant their lips met, colored starbursts lit under his eyelids. A rush of adrenaline surged through his veins, making him feel powerful, invincible and desperate to have her once and for all.

Their kiss yesterday hadn't been nearly enough to quench his thirst for her. It had only made his mouth even drier and more desperate to drink her in again. She was sweet on his tongue, her lips soft and open to him. The small palms of her hands clung to him. The moist, sticky clay felt odd against his skin as it started to dry and tighten, but nothing could ruin the feel of kissing her again.

It was like a dream. He'd stumbled downstairs, half-asleep, to charge his phone. He never expected to find her there at her wheel, looking so serene and focused, so beautiful and determined. Having her in his arms only moments later made him want to pinch himself and ensure he really was awake. It wouldn't be the first dream he'd had about Julianne, although it might be the most realistic.

Julianne bit on his lip, then. The sharp pain made him jerk, the area still sensitive from his previous self-inflicted injury. He pulled away from her, studying her face and coming to terms with the fact that she was real. After all these years she was in his arms again.

"I'm sorry," she said, brushing a gentle fingertip over his lip. "Was that too hard?"

Heath would never admit to that. "You just startled me, that's all."

Julianne nodded, her gaze running over the line of his jaw with a smile curling her lips. Her fingertip scraped over the mix of stubble and clay, making the muscles in his neck tighten and flex with anticipation. "I think we need a shower," she said. "You're a very, very dirty boy."

A shower was an awesome idea. "You make me this way," he replied. With a grin, Heath lifted Julianne up. As tiny as she was, it was nothing to lift her into the air. She wrapped her legs and arms around him, holding him close as he stumbled out of the workshop and headed for the stairs.

When they reached the top of the staircase, her mouth found his again. With one eye on his bedroom up ahead, he stumbled across the landing and through the door. He prayed there weren't any clothes or shoes strewn across the floor to trip him and he was successful. They reached into the bathroom and he pulled one hand away from a firm thigh to switch on the lights.

He expected Julianne to climb down, but she clearly had no intention of letting go of him. Not even to take off their clothes. She refused to take her mouth off of his long enough to see what she was doing.

She reached into the shower, pawing blindly at the knobs until a stream of warm, then hot, water shot from the nozzle. Julianne put her feet down onto the tiles and then stepped backward into the stall, tugging Heath forward until he stumbled and they both slammed against the tile, fully dressed. Their clothes were instantly soaked, and were now transparent and clung to their skin.

Her whole body was on display for him now. Her rosy nipples were hard and thrusting through the damp cotton top. His hands sought them out, crushing them against his palms until her moans echoed off the walls. His mouth dipped down, tugging at her tank top until the peaks of her breasts spilled out over the neckline. He captured one in his mouth, sucking hard.

The hot water ran over their bodies as they touched and tasted each other. Most of the clay was gone now, the faint gray stream of water no longer circling the drain. Their hair was soaking wet, with fat drops of water falling into his eyes as he hovered over her chest. It was getting hard to breathe between the water in his face and the steam in his lungs, but he refused to let go of Julianne long enough to change anything.

A rush of cold air suddenly hit his back as Julianne tugged at his wet shirt. She pulled it over his head and flung it onto the bathroom floor with a wet *thwump*.

"I thought you were tired of me running around without my shirt on," he said with a grin.

"You said it was okay in the shower, remember?"

"That I did." Leaning down, he did the same with her top and her shorts. She was completely exposed to him now, her body a delight for his eyes that had gone so long without gazing upon it. He wanted to take his time, to explore every inch and curve of her, but Julianne wasn't having it. She tugged him back against her, hooking her leg around his hip.

Lifting her into his arms once again, he pressed her back into the corner of the shower, one arm around her waist to support her, the other hand planted firmly on her outer thigh. The hot spray was now running over his back and was no longer on the verge of drowning them.

Julianne's hands reached between them, her fingers finding the waistband of his boxers and pushing them down. He wasn't wearing anything beneath. Without much effort, she'd pushed the shorts low on his hips and exposed him. He expected her to touch him then, but instead, she stiffened slightly in his arms.

"Heath?"

Julianne's voice was small, competing with the loud rush of the shower and the heavy panting of their breaths, but he heard her. He stopped, his hands mere inches from the moist heat between her thighs.

She wasn't changing her mind again, was she? He wasn't sure he could take that a second time. "Yes?"

"Before we…" Her voice trailed off. Her golden brown lashes were dark and damp, but still full enough to hide her eyes from him. "I don't want to tell anyone about us. *This*. Not yet."

Heath tried not to let the hard bite of her words affect him. She kept insisting she wasn't embarrassed of him and yet she repeatedly went out of her way to prove otherwise. He wanted to ask why. To push her for more information, but this wasn't exactly the right moment to have an in-depth relationship discussion. What was he going to say? He was wedged between her thighs, his pants shoved low on his hips. Now was not the time to disagree with her. At least not if he ever wanted to sleep with his wife.

"Okay," he agreed and her body relaxed. He waited only a moment before sliding his hand the rest of the way up her thigh. His fingers found her slick and warm, her loud cry more evidence that she wanted him and was ready to have him at last. He grazed over her flesh, moving in sure, firm strokes, effectively ending the conversation.

Julianne arched her back, pressing her hips hard into his hand and crying out. Her worries of a moment ago vanished and he intended to plow full steam ahead before she changed her mind, this time for good.

Heath braced her hips in his hands, lifting her up, and then stopping just as he pushed against the entrance to her body. He didn't want to move at this snail's pace; he wanted to dive hard and fast into her, but a part of him kept waiting for her to stop him. He clenched his jaw, praying for self-control and the ability to pull away when she asked.

"Yes, Heath," she whispered. "Please. We've waited this long, don't make me wait any longer."

Heath eased his hips forward and before he knew it, he was buried deep inside her. That realization forced his eyes closed and his body stiff as a shudder of pleasure moved through him. Pressing his face into her shoulder, he reveled in the long-awaited sensation of Julianne's welcoming heat wrapped around him.

How many years, nights, days, had he fantasized about the moment that had been stolen away from him? And now he had her at last. He almost couldn't believe it. It was the middle of the night. Maybe this was all just some wild dream. There was only one way to test it.

Withdrawing slowly, he thrust hard and quick, drawing a sharp cry from her and a low growl of satisfaction from his own throat. He could feel Julianne's fingers pressing insistently into his back, the muscles of her sex tightening around him. He was most certainly awake. And there was no more reason to hold back.

Heath gripped her tightly, leaning in to pin her securely to the wall. And then he moved in her. What started as a slow savoring of her body quickly morphed into a fierce claiming. Julianne clung to him, taking everything he had to give and answering his every thrust with a roll of her hips and a gasp of pleasure.

Everything about this moment felt so incredibly right. It wasn't romantic or sweet. It was fierce and raw, but that was what it needed to be. After eleven years of waiting... eleven years of other lovers who never quite met the standard Julianne had set. He was like a starving man at a buffet. He couldn't get enough of her fast enough to satiate the need that had built in him all these years.

Yet even as he pumped into her, his mind drifted to that night—the night they should have shared together in Gibraltar. They should have been each other's first. It would have been special and important and everything he'd built up in his mind. Instead, he'd given it up to some sorority girl whose name he barely remembered anymore. He didn't know who Julianne finally chose to be her first lover, but even all these years later, he was fiercely jealous of that man for taking what he felt was his.

He was going to make himself crazy with thoughts like that. To purge his brain, he sought out her mouth. He focused on the taste of her, instead. The slide of her tongue along his own. The sharp edge of her teeth nipping at him. The hollow echo of her cries inside his head.

His fingers pressed harder into the plump flesh of her backside, holding her as he surged forward, pounding relentlessly into her body. Julianne tore her mouth from his. The faster he moved, the louder Julianne's gasps of "yes, yes" were in his ear. He lost himself in pleasure, feeling her body tense and tighten around him as she neared her release.

When she started to shudder in his arms, he eased back and opened his eyes. He wanted to see this moment and remember it forever. Her head was thrown back and her eyes closed. Her mouth fell open, her groans and gasps escalating into loud screams. "Heath, yes, Heath!" she shouted.

It was the most erotic sound he'd ever heard. The sound went straight to his brain, the surge of his own pleasure shooting down his spine and exploding into his own release. He poured into her, his groans mixing with hers and the roar of the pounding water.

At last, he thought as he reached out to turn off the water. He'd waited years for this moment and it was greater than he ever could have anticipated.

Seven

He signed them.

Well, if that wasn't the cherry on top, Julianne didn't know what was. She didn't know exactly when it happened, but as she sat down at the kitchen table the next morning, she noticed the divorce papers were out of the envelope. She flipped through the bound pages to the one tabbed by her attorney. There she found Heath's signature, large and sharply scrawled across the page beside yesterday's date.

Well, at least he had signed it *before* they had sex.

That didn't make her feel much better, though. She had already woken up feeling awkward about what happened between them. She'd crept out of his bed as quietly as she could and escaped to the safety of downstairs.

Their frantic lovemaking in the middle of the night certainly wasn't planned. Or well-thought-out. It also wasn't anything she intended to repeat. He'd caught her in a vulnerable moment. Somehow, at 3:00 a.m., all the reasons it seemed like a bad idea faded away. Well, they were all back now. Eleven years' worth of reasons, starting with why they'd never had sex in the first place and ending with that phone call to his "sweetheart" the other night. They weren't going to be together. Last night was a one-time thing.

But even then, coming downstairs and finding their signed divorce papers on the table felt like a slap across the face somehow.

This was why she'd asked him to keep this all a secret. There was no sense in drawing anyone else into the drama of their relationship when the odds were that it would all be over before long. No matter what happened between them last night, they were heading for a divorce. He'd said that he didn't want a divorce, he wanted her to choose. Apparently that wasn't entirely true. For all his sharp accusations, he seemed to want to have his cake and eat it as well.

With a sigh, she sipped her coffee and considered her options. She could get upset, but that wouldn't do much good. She was the one who had the papers drawn up, albeit as a result of his goading. She couldn't very well hold a grudge against him for signing them after she'd had them overnighted to the house.

As she did when she got stuck on one of her sculptures, she decided it was best to sit back and try to look at this situation from a different angle. She and Heath were getting a divorce. It was a long time coming and nothing was going to change that now. With that in mind, what did sleeping with Heath hurt? She'd always wanted him. He'd always wanted her. Their unfinished wedding night had been like a dark cloud hovering overhead for the last eleven years.

When she thought about it that way, perhaps it was just something they needed to do. Things might be a little awkward between them, but they hadn't exactly been hunky-dory before.

Now that they'd gotten it out of their system, they could move forward with clear heads. But move forward into what? The divorce seemed to be a hot-button issue. Once that was official and they stopped fighting, what would happen? There was a chemistry between them that was impossible to deny. Now that they'd crossed the line, she imagined that it would be hard not to do it again.

What if they did?

Julianne wasn't sure. It didn't seem like the best idea. And yet, she wasn't quite ready to give it up. Last night had been…amazing. Eleven years in the making and worth the wait. It made her angry. It was bad enough that Tommy had attacked her and she had the shadow of his death on her conscience. But the impact had been so long-lasting. What if her wedding night with Heath had gone the way it should have? What if they'd been able to come home and tell their parents and be together? She felt like even long after he was dead, Tommy had taken not only her innocence, but also her future and happiness with Heath.

Back in college when her mind went down into this dark spiral, her therapist would tell her she couldn't change the past. All she could do was guide her future. There was no sense dwelling on what had happened. "Accept, acknowledge and grow" was her therapist's motto.

Applied to this instance, she had to accept that she'd had sex with Heath. She acknowledged that it was amazing. To grow, she needed to decide if she wanted to do it again and what the consequences would be. Why did there have to be negative consequences? It was just sex, right? They could do it twice or twenty times, but if she kept that in perspective, things would be fine. It didn't mean anything, at least not to her. Since he had signed the divorce papers first, she'd have to assume he felt the same way.

In fact... Julianne reached for the divorce decree and the pen lying there. She turned back to the flagged page and the blank line for her signature. With only a moment's hesitation, she put her pen to the paper and scrawled her signature beside his.

"See?" she said aloud to the empty room. "It didn't mean anything."

There. It was done. All she had to do was drop it back in the mail to her lawyer. She shoved the paperwork back in the envelope and set it aside. For a moment, there was the euphoria of having the weight of their marriage lifted from her shoulders. It didn't last long, however. It was quickly followed by the sinking feeling of failure in her stomach.

With a groan, she pushed away her coffee. She needed to get out of the bunkhouse. Running a few errands would help clear her mind. She could stop by the post office and mail the paperwork, pick up a few things at the store and go by the hospital to see Dad. Her kiln wouldn't be delivered until later in the afternoon, so why not? Sitting around waiting for Heath to wake up felt odd. There was no reason to make last night seem more important than it was. She would treat it like any other hookup.

She found it was a surprisingly sunny and warm day for early October. That wouldn't last. The autumn leaves on the trees were past their prime and would drop to the ground dead before long. They'd have their first snow within a few weeks, she was certain.

She took advantage of the weather, putting the top down on her convertible. There would still be a cold sting to her cheeks, but she didn't mind. She wanted the wind in her hair. Pulling out of the drive, she headed west for the hospital. With all the work on her studio, she hadn't been to see her father for a couple days. Now was a good time. Molly's car was at the house, so Dad was alone and they could chat without other people around. Even though her father didn't—and couldn't—know the details of what was bothering her, he had a calming effect on her that would help.

She checked in at the desk to see what room he was in now that he was out of intensive care, and then headed up to the fourth floor. Ken was sitting up when she arrived, watching television and poking at his food tray with dismay.

"Morning, Dad."

A smile immediately lit his face. He was a little thinner and he looked tired, but his color was better and they'd taken him off most of the monitors. "Morning, June-bug. You didn't happen to bring me a sausage biscuit, did you?"

Julianne gave him a gentle hug and sat down at the foot of his bed. "Dad, you just had open-heart surgery. A sausage biscuit? Really?"

"Well…" He shrugged, poking at his food again. "It's better than this stuff. I don't even know what this is."

Julianne leaned over his tray. "It looks like scrambled egg whites, oatmeal, cantaloupe and dry toast."

"It all tastes like wallpaper paste to me. No salt, no sugar, no fat, no flavor. Why did they bother saving me, really?"

Julianne frowned. "You may not like it, but you've got to eat healthier. You promised me you'd live to at least ninety and I expect you to hold up your end of the bargain."

Ken sighed and put a bite of oatmeal in his mouth with a grimace. "I'm only doing this for your sake."

"When do you get to come home? I'm sure Mom's version of healthy food will be better tasting."

"Tomorrow, thank goodness. I'm so relieved to skip the rehab facility. You and I both know it's really a nursing home. I might be near death, but I'm not ready for that, yet."

"I'm glad. I didn't want you there, either."

"Your mother says that you and Heath are both staying in the bunkhouse."

"Yes," she said with a curt nod. She didn't dare elaborate. The only person who could read her better than Heath was her dad. He would pick up on something pretty easily.

"How's that going? You two haven't spent that much time together in a long while. You were inseparable as kids."

Julianne shrugged. "It's been fine." She picked up the plastic pitcher of ice water and poured herself a glass. Driving with the top down always made her thirsty. "I think we're both getting a feel for one another again."

"You know," he said, putting his spoon back down on his tray, "I always thought you two might end up together."

The water in her mouth shot into different directions as she sputtered, some going into her lungs, some threatening to shoot out her nose. She set the cup down, coughing furiously for a few moments until her eyes were teary and her face was red.

"You okay?" he asked.

"Went down the wrong way," she whispered between coughs. "I'm fine. Sorry. What, uh…what makes you say something like that?"

"I don't know. You two always seemed to complement each other nicely. Neither of you seem to be able to find the right person. I've always wondered if you weren't looking in the wrong places."

This was an unexpected conversation. She wasn't entirely sure how to respond to it. "Looking in the family is frowned on, Dad."

"Oh, come on," he muttered irritably. "You're not related. You never even lived in the same house, really. It's more like falling for the boy next door."

"You don't think it would be weird?"

"Your mother and I want to see you and Heath happy. If it turns out you're happy together, then that's the way it is."

"What if it didn't work out? It's not like I can just change my number and pretend Heath doesn't exist after we break up."

Ken frowned and narrowed his eyes at her. "Do you always go into your relationships figuring out how you'll handle it when they end? That's not very optimistic."

"No, but it's practical. You've seen my track record."

"I have. Your mother told me the last one didn't end well."

He didn't know the half of it. "Why would dating Heath be any different? I mean, if he were even remotely interested, and I'm certain he's not."

Her father's blue-gray eyes searched her face for a moment, then he leaned back against the pillows. "I remember when you were little and you came home from school one day all breathless with excitement. You climbed into my lap and whispered in my ear that you'd kissed a boy on the playground. You had Heath's name doodled all over the inside of your unicorn notebook."

"Dad, I was nine."

"I know that. And I was twelve when I first kissed your mother at the junior high dance. I knew then that I was going to be with her for the rest of my life. I just had to convince her."

"She wasn't as keen on the idea?"

Ken shrugged. "She just needed a little persuading. Molly was beautiful, just like you are. She had her choice of boys in school. I just had to make sure she knew I was the best one. By our senior year in high school, I had won her over. I proposed that summer after we graduated and the rest is history."

Julianne felt a touch of shame for not knowing that much about her parents' early relationship. She had no idea they'd met so young and got engaged right out of school. They were married nearly ten years before they finally had her, so somehow, it hadn't registered in her mind. "You were so young. How did you know you were making the right choice?"

"I loved your mother. It might not have been the easy choice to get married so young, but we made the most of it. On our wedding day, I promised your mother a fairy tale. Making good on that promise keeps me working at our marriage every day. There were hard times and times when we fought and times when we both thought it was a colossal mistake. But that's when you've got to fight harder to keep what you want."

Julianne's mind went to the package of paperwork in her bag and she immediately felt guilty. The one thing she never did was fight for her relationship with Heath. She had wanted it, but at the same time, she didn't think she could have it. Tommy had left her in shreds. It took a lot of years and a lot of counseling to get where she was now and, admittedly, that wasn't even the healthiest of places. She was a relationship failure who had just slept with her husband for the first time in their eleven-year marriage.

Maybe if things had been different. Maybe if Heath's parents hadn't died. Or if Tommy hadn't come to the farm. Maybe then they could have been happy together, the way her father envisioned.

"I'll keep that in mind when I'm ready to get back in the saddle," she said, trying not to sound too dismissive.

Ken smiled and patted her hand. "I'm an old man who's only loved one woman his whole life. What do I know about relationships? Speaking of which—" he turned toward the door and grinned widely "—it's time for my sponge bath."

Julianne turned to look at the door and was relieved to find her mother there instead of a young nurse. "Well, you two have fun," she laughed. "I'll see you tomorrow at the house."

She gave her mom a quick hug and made her way out of the hospital. Putting the top up on the convertible, she drove faster than usual, trying to put some miles between her and her father's words.

He couldn't be right about her relationship with Heath. If he knew everything that had happened, her father would realize that it just wasn't meant to be. They would never be happy together and she had the divorce papers to prove it.

Julianne cruised back into town, rolling past Daisy's Diner and the local bar, the Wet Hen. Just beyond them were the market and the tiny post office. No one was in line in front of her, so she was able to fill out the forms and get the paperwork overnighted back to her lawyer's office.

It wasn't until she handed over the envelope and the clerk tossed it into the back room that her father's words echoed in her head and she felt a pang of regret. She hadn't fought. She'd just ended it. A large part of her life had been spent with Heath as her husband. It wasn't a traditional marriage by any stretch, but it had been a constant throughout the hectic ups and downs of her life.

"Ma'am?" the clerk asked. "Are you okay? Did you need something else?"

Julianne looked up at him. For a brief second, the words *I changed my mind* were on the tip of her tongue. He would fetch it back for her. She could wait. She wasn't entirely certain that she wanted this.

But Heath did. He wanted his freedom, she could tell.

She'd left him hanging for far, far too long. He deserved to find a woman who would love him and give him the life and family he desired. Maybe Miss Caribbean could give him that. That was what she'd intended when she broke it off with him originally. To give him that chance. She just hadn't had the strength to cut the last tie and give up on them.

It was time, no matter what her dad said. "No," she said with a smile and a shake of her head. "I'm fine. I was just trying to remember if I needed stamps, but I don't. Thank you."

Turning on her heel, she rushed out of the post office and back out onto the street.

Heath was not surprised to wake up alone, but it still irritated him. He wandered through the quiet house and realized at last that her car was not in the driveway. It wasn't hard to figure out that last night's tryst had not sat well with her. As with most things, it seemed like a good idea at the time.

They had been on the same page in the moment. It had been hot. More erotic than he ever dared imagine. They fell back to sleep in each other's arms. He'd dozed off cautiously optimistic that he might get some morning lovin' as well. That, obviously, had not panned out, but again, he was not surprised.

Frankly, he was more surprised they'd had sex to begin with. He dangled the bait but never expected her to bite. His plan had always been to push their hot-button issue, make her uncomfortable and get her to finally file for divorce. He never anticipated rubbing clay all over her body and having steamy shower sex in the middle of the night. That was the stuff of his hottest fantasies.

Of course, he'd also never thought she would cave so

quickly to the pressure and order the divorce paperwork the same day he demanded it. He expected spending weeks, even months wearing her down. She had already held out eleven years. Then the papers arrived with such speed that he almost didn't believe it. He'd wanted movement, one way or another, so he figured he should sign them before she changed her mind again.

Sleeping with her a few hours later was an unanticipated complication.

Heath glanced over at the table where he'd left the papers. They were gone. He frowned. Maybe she wanted this divorce more than he'd thought. He'd obviously given her the push she needed to make it happen, and she'd run straight to the post office with her prize.

He opted not to dwell on any of it. He signed, so he couldn't complain if she did the same. What was done was done. Besides, that's not why he was here anyway. Heath had come to the farm, first and foremost, to take care of things while Ken recovered. Dealing with Julianne and their divorce was a secondary task.

Returning to his room, he got dressed in some old jeans, a long-sleeved flannel shirt and his work boots. When he was ready he opted to head out to the fields in search of Owen, the farm's only full-time employee. It didn't take long. He just had to hop on one of the four-wheelers and follow the sound of the chain saw. They were in the final stretch leading up to Christmas-tree season, so it was prep time.

He found Owen in the west fields. The northern part of the property was too heavily sloped for people to pick and cut their own trees. The trees on that side were harvested and provided to the local tree lots and hardware stores for sale. Not everyone enjoyed a trek through the cold to find the perfect tree, although Heath couldn't fathom why. The tree lots didn't have Molly's hot chocolate or sleigh rides with carols and Christmas lights. No atmosphere at all.

Most of the pick-and-cut trees were on the west side of the property. The western fields were on flat, easy terrain and they were closest to the shop and the bagging station. He found Owen cutting low branches off the trees and tying bright red ribbons on the branches.

At any one time on the farm there were trees in half a dozen states of growth, from foot-tall saplings to fifteen-year-old giants that would be put in local shopping centers and town squares. At around eight years with proper trimming, a tree was perfect for the average home; full, about six to seven feet tall and sturdy enough to hold heavier ornaments. The red ribbons signified to their customers that the tree was ready for harvest.

"Morning, Owen."

The older man looked up from his work and gave a wave. He put down the chain saw and slipped off one glove to shake Heath's hand. "Morning there, Heath. Are you joining me today?"

"I am. It looks like we're prepping trees."

"That we are." Owen lifted his Patriots ball cap and smoothed his thinning gray hair beneath it before fitting it back on his head. "I've got another chain saw for you on the back of my ATV. Did you bring your work gloves and some protective gear?"

Heath whipped a pair of gloves out of his back pocket and smiled. He had his goggles and ear protection in the tool chest bolted to the back of the four-wheeler. "It hasn't been so long that I'd forget the essentials."

"I don't know," Owen laughed. "Not a lot of need for work gloves in fancy Manhattan offices."

"Some days, I could use the ear protection."

Owen smiled and handed over the chain saw to Heath. "I'm working my way west. Most of this field to the right will be ready for Christmas. Back toward the house still needs a year or two more to grow. You still know how to tell which ones are ready for cutting?"

He did. When he was too young to use the chainsaw, he was out in the fields tying ribbons and shaping trees with hedge clippers. "I've got it, Owen."

Heath went off into the opposite direction Owen was working so they covered more territory. With his headset and goggles in place, he cranked up the chain saw and started making his way through the trees. It was therapeutic to do some physical work. He didn't really get the chance to get dirty anymore. He'd long ago lost the calluses on his hands. His clothes never smelled of pine or had stains from tree sap. It was nice to get back to the work he knew.

There was nothing but the buzz of the saw, the cold sting of the air, the sharp scent of pine and the crunch of dirt and twigs under his boots. He lost himself in the rhythm of his work. It gave him a much-needed outlet as well. He was able to channel some of his aggression and irritation at Julianne through the power tool.

His mind kept going back to their encounter and the look on her face when she'd asked him to keep their relationship a secret. Like it had ever been anything but a secret. Did she think that once they had sex he would dash out of the house and run screaming through the trees that he'd slept with her at last? Part of him had felt like that after finally achieving such an important milestone in their marriage, but given he'd signed the divorce papers only a few hours before that, it didn't seem appropriate.

It irritated him that she wouldn't just admit the truth.

She would go through the whole song and dance of excuses for her behavior but refused to just say out loud that she was embarrassed to be with him. She wanted him, but she didn't want anyone to know it.

Up until that moment in the shower, he'd thought perhaps that wasn't an issue for them anymore. She might not want people to know they eloped as teenagers, but now? Julianne had been quick to point out earlier in the night just how "successful" he was. He had his regrets in life, but she was right. He wasn't exactly a bad catch. He was a slippery one, as some women had discovered, but not a bad one.

And yet, it still wasn't enough for her. What did she want from him? And why did he even care?

He was over her. Over. And he had been for quite some time. He'd told Nolan he didn't love her anymore and that was true. There was an attraction there, but it was a biological impulse he couldn't rid himself of. The sex didn't change anything. They were simply settling a long overdue score between them.

That just left him with a big "now what?" He had no clue. If she were off mailing their divorce papers, the clock was ticking. There were only thirty or so days left in their illustrious marriage. That was what he wanted, right? He started this because he wanted his freedom.

Heath set down the chain saw and pulled a bundle of red ribbons out of his back pocket. He doubled back over the trees he'd trimmed, tying ribbons on the branches with clumsy fingers that were numb from the vibration of the saw.

He didn't really know what he wanted or what he was doing with his life anymore. All he knew was that he wasn't going to let Julianne run away from him this time.

They were going to talk about this whether she liked it or not. It probably wouldn't change things. It might not even get her back in his bed again. But somehow, some way, he just knew that their marriage needed to end with a big bang.

Eight

Julianne returned to an empty bunkhouse. The Porsche wasn't in the driveway. She breathed a sigh of relief and went inside, stopping short when she saw the yellow piece of paper on the kitchen table. Picking it up, she read over the hard block letters of Heath's penmanship.

There's a sushi restaurant in Danbury on the square called Lotus. I have reservations there tonight at seven.

With a sigh, she dropped the note back to the table. Heath didn't ask her to join him. He wasn't concerned about whether or not she might have plans or even if she didn't *want* to have dinner with him. It didn't matter. This was a summons and she would be found in contempt if she didn't show up.

Julianne knew immediately that she should not have run

out on him this morning. They should have talked about it, about what it meant and what was going to happen going forward. Instead, she bailed. He was irritated with her and she didn't blame him. That didn't mean she appreciated having her evening dictated to her, but the idea of some good sushi was a lure. She hadn't had any in a while. Daisy's Diner wasn't exactly known for their fresh sashimi.

She checked the time on her phone. It was four-thirty now and it took about forty-five minutes to drive to Danbury. She'd never been to Lotus, but she'd heard of it before. It was upscale. She would have just enough time to get ready. She hadn't exactly gone all-out this morning to run some errands around town, so she was starting from scratch.

Julianne quickly showered and washed her hair. She blew it dry and put it up in hot rollers to set while she did her makeup and searched her closet for something to wear. For some reason, this felt like a date. Given they'd filed for divorce today, it also felt a little absurd, but she couldn't stop herself from adding those extra special touches to her makeup. After a week surrounded by nothing but trees and dirt, the prospect of dressing up and going out was intriguing.

Except she had nothing to wear. She didn't exactly have a lot of fancy clothes. She spent most of her time covered in mud with a ponytail. Reaching into the back of the closet, she found her all-purpose black dress. It was the simple, classic little black dress that she used for various gallery showings and events. It was knee length and fitted with a deep V-neck and three-quarter sleeves. A black satin belt wrapped around the waist, giving it a little bit of shine and luxury without being a rhinestone-covered sparklefest.

It was classic, simple and understated, and it showed off her legs. She paired it with pointy-toed patent leather heels and a silver medallion necklace that rested right in the hollow between her collarbones.

By the time she shook out the curls in her hair, relaxing them into soft waves, and applied perfume at her pulse points, it was time to leave.

She was anxious as she drove down the winding two-lane highway to Danbury. The fall evening light was nearly gone as she arrived in town. The small square was the center of college nightlife in Danbury and included several bars, restaurants and other hangouts. Lotus was at a small but upper-end location. She imagined it was where the college kids saved up to go for nice dates or where parents took them for graduation dinners and weekend visits.

Julianne parked her convertible a few spots down from Heath's silver Porsche. He was standing outside the restaurant, paying more attention to his phone than to the people and activities going on around him.

She took her time getting out of the car so she could enjoy the view without him knowing it. He was wearing a dark gray suit with a platinum dress shirt and diamond-patterned tie of gray, black and blue. The suit fit him immaculately, stretching across his wide shoulders and tapering into his narrow waist.

Heath had a runner's physique; slim, but hard as a rock. Touching him in that shower had been a fantasy come true after watching those carved abs from a distance day after day. Her only regret had been the rush. Their encounter had been a mad frenzy of need and possession. There was no time for exploring and savoring the way she wanted to. And if she had any sense, there never would be. Last night was a moment of weakness, a settling of scores.

It was then that Heath looked up and saw her loitering beside the Camaro. He smiled for an instant when he saw her but quickly wiped away the expression to a polite but neutral face. It was as though he was happy to see her but didn't want her to know. Or he kept forgetting he shouldn't be happy to see her. Their relationship was so complicated.

Julianne approached him, keeping her own face cautiously blank. She had been summoned, after all. This was not a date. It was a reckoning. "I'm here, as requested," she said.

Heath nodded and slipped his phone into his inner breast pocket. "So you are. I'm mildly surprised." He reached for the door to the restaurant and held it open for her to go inside ahead of him.

She tried not to take offense. He implied she was flaky somehow. After eleven years of artfully dodging divorce, it probably looked that way from the outside. "We've got weeks together ahead of us, Heath. There's no sense in starting off on the wrong foot."

The maître d' took their names and led them to their table. As they walked through the dark space, Heath leaned into her and whispered in her ear. "We didn't start off on the wrong foot," he said. The low rumble of his voice in her ear sent a shiver racing through her body. "We started off on the absolutely right foot."

"And then we filed for divorce," she quipped, pulling away before she got sucked into his tractor beam.

Heath chuckled, following quietly behind her. They were escorted to a leather booth in the corner opposite a large column that housed a salt water fish tank. The cylinder glowed blue in the dark room, one of three around the restaurant that seemed to hold the roof up overhead. The tanks were brimming with life, peppered with anemones, urchins, clown fish and other bright, tropical fish. They were the only lights in the restaurant aside from the individual spotlights that illuminated each table.

They settled in, placing their drink orders and coming

to an agreement on the assortment of sushi pieces they'd like to share. Once that was done, there was nothing to do but face why they were here.

"You're probably wondering what this is about," Heath said after sipping his premium sake.

"You mean you're not just hungry?" Julianne retorted, knowing full well that he had bigger motivations than food on his mind.

"We needed to talk about last night. I thought getting away from home and all *those people*," he said with emphasis, "that you worry about seeing us together might help."

Julianne sighed. He'd taken it personally last night when she asked to keep their encounter a secret. She could tell by the downturn of his lips when he said "those people." He didn't understand. "Heath, I'm not—"

He held up his hand. "It's fine, Jules. You don't want anyone seeing us together. I get it. Nothing has changed since we were eighteen. I should just be happy we finally slept together. Unfortunately, finding you gone when I woke up put a sour taste in my mouth."

"And going downstairs to find you'd signed the divorce papers left a bitter taste in mine."

Heath's eyes narrowed at her for a moment before he relaxed back against the seat. "I signed those last night after you left me on the couch, alone and wanting you once again. I assure you that making love to you in the shower at three a.m. was not in my plan at the time."

Julianne shook her head. "It doesn't matter, Heath. We both know it's what we need to do. What we've needed to do for a very long time. I'm sorry to have drawn it out as long as I have. It wasn't very considerate of me to put you through that. The papers are signed and mailed. It's done. Now we can just relax. We don't have to fight about it anymore. The pressure is off and we can focus on the farm and helping Dad recuperate."

He watched her speak, his gaze focused on her lips, but he didn't seem to have the posture of relief she expected. He had started all this after all. He'd virtually bullied her into filing. Now he seemed displeased by it all.

"So," she asked, "are you upset with me because I did what you asked? Because I'm confused."

Heath sighed. "I'm not upset with you, Jules. You're right, you did exactly as I asked. We filed. That's what we needed to do. I guess I'm just not sure what last night was about. Or why you took off like a criminal come morning."

Julianne looked at him, searching his hazel eyes. Having a relationship with him was so complicated. She wanted him, but she couldn't truly have him. Not when the truth about what had happened that night with Tommy still loomed between them. She didn't want anyone else to have him, either, but she felt guilty about keeping him from happiness. Letting him go didn't seem to make him happy. What the hell was she supposed to do?

"We shouldn't read too much into last night," she said at last. "It was sex. Great sex that was long overdue. I don't regret doing it, despite what you seem to think. I just didn't feel like psychoanalyzing it this morning, especially with our divorce papers sitting beside my cup of coffee."

"So you thought the sex was great?" Heath smiled and arched his brow conspiratorially.

"Is that all you got out of that?" Julianne sighed. "It was great, yes. But it doesn't have to change everything and it doesn't have to mean anything, either. We're attracted to each other. We always have been. Anything more than that is where we run into a problem. So can't it just be a fun outlet for years of pent-up attraction?"

Heath eyed her for a moment, his brows drawn together

in thought. "So you're saying that last night wasn't a big deal? I agree. Does that mean you're wanting to continue this…uh…*relationship?*"

When she woke up this morning, it didn't seem like the right thing to do. It would complicate things further in her opinion. But here, in a dark restaurant with moody lighting and a handsome Heath sitting across from her, it wasn't such a bad idea anymore. They were getting a divorce. The emotional heartstrings had been cut once and for all. If they both knew what they were getting into, why not have a little fun?

"We're both adults. We know that it's just physical. The things that held me back in our youth would not be in play here. So, perhaps."

The waiter approached the table with two large platters of assorted sushi. Heath watched only Julianne as things were rearranged and placed in front of them. The heat of his gaze traveled like a warm caress along her throat to the curve of her breasts. She felt a blush rise to her cheeks and chest from his extensive inventory of her assets.

When the waiter finally disappeared, Heath spoke. "You want us to have a fling?"

That's what she'd just suggested, hadn't she? Maybe that was what they needed. A no-strings outlet for their sexual tension. Perhaps then, she could sate her desire for Heath without having to cross the personal boundaries that kept them apart. He never needed to know about the night with Tommy or what happened during their botched honeymoon. She could make it up to him in the weeks that followed.

And why not? They were still married, weren't they?

Julianne smiled and reached for her chopsticks. She plucked a piece from the platter and put it into her mouth. Her eyes never left his even as she slipped her foot out of her shoe and snaked it beneath the table in search of his leg. His eyes widened as her toes found his ankle beneath the cuff of his suit pants. She slid them higher, caressing the tense muscles of his calves. By the time she reached his inner thigh, he was white-knuckling the table.

She happily chewed, continuing to eat as though her foot had not just made contact with the firm heat of his desire beneath the table. "You'd better eat. I can't finish all this sushi on my own," she said, smiling innocently.

"Jules," he whispered, closing his eyes and absorbing the feeling as her toes glided along the length of him. "Jules!" he repeated, his eyes flying open. "Please," he implored. "I get it. The answer is yes. Let's either eat dinner or leave, but please put your shoe back on. It's a long drive home in separate cars. Don't torture me."

The next few weeks went by easily. The uproar of the move and chaos of being thrown together after so long apart had finally dissipated. Dad was home and doing well under Nurse Lynn's care. Jules had a fully operational workshop with her new kiln. She had three new gallery pieces in various stages of completion that were showing a lot of potential and nearly a full shelving unit of stoneware for her shop. During the day, she worked with Molly in the Christmas store preparing for the upcoming holiday rush. They made wreaths, stocked shelves and handled the paperwork the farm generated. In the evenings, she worked on her art.

Heath had done much the same. During the day, he was out in the fields working with Owen. He'd sent out some feelers for teenagers to work part-time starting at Thanksgiving and had gotten a couple of promising responses. When the sun went down, he worked on his computer, trying to stay up-to-date with emails and other business issues. Things seemed to be going fine as best he could tell.

Most nights, Julianne would slip into his bed. Some encounters were fevered and rushed, others were leisurely and stretched long into the early hours of the morning. He'd indulged his every fantasy where she was concerned, filling his cup with Julianne so he would have no regrets when all of this was over.

He usually found himself alone come morning. Julianne told him she woke up with bad dreams nearly every night, although she wouldn't elaborate. When she did wake up, she went downstairs to work. When she returned to bed, she went to her own room. It was awkward to fall asleep with her almost every night and wake up alone just as often.

Despite the comfortable rhythm they'd developed, moments like that were enough to remind him that things were not as sublime as they seemed. He was not, at long last, in a relationship with Julianne. What they had was physical, with a strong barrier in place to keep her emotions in check. She was still holding back, the way she always had. Their discussions never strayed to their marriage, their past, or their future. She avoided casual, physical contact with him throughout the day. When nightfall came, they were simply reaping the benefits of their marriage while they could.

Given Heath had spent eleven years trying to get this far, he couldn't complain much. But it did bother him from time to time. When he woke up alone. When he wanted to kiss her, but Molly or Nurse Lynn were nearby and she would shy away. When he remembered the clock was ticking down on their divorce.

At the same time, things at the bunkhouse had certainly been far more peaceful than he'd ever anticipated going into this scenario. It was one of those quiet evenings when his phone rang. He'd just gotten out of the shower after a long day of working outside and had settled in front of his laptop when the music of his phone caught his attention from the coffee table.

Heath reached for his phone and frowned. It was Nolan's number and picture on the screen of his smartphone. He was almost certain this wouldn't be a social call. With a sigh, he hit the button to answer. "Hey."

"I'm sorry," Nolan began, making Heath grit his teeth. "I had to call."

"What is it?" And why couldn't Nolan handle it? He couldn't voice the query aloud. Nolan was running the whole show to accommodate Heath's family emergency, but Heath couldn't help the irritation creeping up his spine. He had enough to worry about in Connecticut without New York's troubles creeping in.

"Madame Badeau called today. And yesterday. And last week. For some reason, she must think your assistant is lying about you being out of the office. She finally threw a fit and insisted to talk to me."

Heath groaned aloud. Thank goodness only Nolan and his assistant had his personal number. The older French woman refused to use email, so if she had his personal number, she'd call whenever she felt the urge, time difference be damned. "What does she want?"

Nolan chuckled softly on the line. "Aside from you?"

"Most especially," Heath responded..

"She wants you in Paris this weekend."

"What?" It was *Wednesday*. Was she insane? He held her advertising account; he wasn't hers to summon at her whim. "Why?"

"She's unhappy with the European campaign we put together. You and I both know she approved it and seemed happy when we first presented it, but she's had a change of heart. It's a last-minute modification and she wants you there to personally oversee it. She wants the commercial reshot, the print ads redone—everything."

That wasn't a weekend task. Heath smelled a rat. Surely she wasn't just using this as an excuse to lure him to Paris. He'd told her he was married. She seemed to understand. "Why can't Mickey handle this?" Mickey was their art director. He was the one who usually handled the shoots. Redoing the J'Adore campaign fell solidly into Mickey's bucket.

"She didn't like his vision. She wants you there and no one else. I was worried about this. I'm sorry, but there's no dissuading her. I told her about your leave of absence for a family emergency, but it didn't make any difference to her. All she said was that she'd send her private jet to expedite the trip and get you back home as quickly as possible. A long weekend at the most, she insisted."

As much as Heath would like to take that private jet and tell Cecilia what she could do with it, they needed her account. It was hugely profitable for them. If she pulled out after they had spent the last two years making J'Adore the most sought-after cosmetic line in the market, it would be catastrophic. Not only would they lose her account, but others would also wonder why she left and might consider jumping ship. It was too high-profile to ruin. That meant Heath was going to Paris. Just perfect.

"So when is the plane arriving to pick me up?"

"Thursday afternoon in Hartford. Wheels up at four."

"I guess I'll pack my bags. I didn't really bring a lot of my suits to work on the farm. Thankfully it's only for a few days."

"You need to pack Julianne's bags, too."

"What?" he yelled into the phone. "How the hell did she get involved in this discussion?"

"Just relax," Nolan insisted, totally unfazed by Heath's tone. "When I was trying to talk her out of summoning you, I told her that your father-in-law had a heart attack and you and Julianne had gone to the farm. I thought reminding her about your wife and the serious situation you were dealing with would cool her off a little. I lost my mind and thought she would be a reasonable person. Instead, she insisted you bring Julianne to Paris as well."

"Why would I want to bring her with me?"

"Why wouldn't you want to bring your sweet, beloved wife with you to Paris? It's romantic," Nolan said, "and it would be suspicious if you didn't want to bring her. Between you and me, I think Madame Badeau wants to see her competition in the flesh. What can it hurt? Maybe she'll back off for good once she sees Julianne and realizes she's not just a made-up relationship to keep her at arm's length."

Heath groaned again. He'd never met a woman this aggressive. Had his mother not died when he was a child, she would be a year younger than Cecilia. It didn't make a difference to her. She was a wealthy, powerful woman who was used to getting what she wanted, including a steady stream of young lovers. Heath was just a shiny toy she wanted because she couldn't have him.

"Do you really think it will help to take her?"

"I do. And look at the bright side. You'll get a nice weekend in Paris. You'll be flying on a fancy private jet and staying in a fabulous hotel along the Seine. It's not the biggest imposition in the world. You're probably tired of staring at pine trees by now. It's been almost a month since you went up there."

Heath *was* tired of the trees. Well, that wasn't entirely

correct. He was tired of being cooped up here, pacing around like a caged tiger. If it weren't for the nights with Julianne to help him blow off steam, he might've gone stir-crazy by now. Perhaps a weekend away would give him the boost he needed to make it through the holidays. It was early November, so better now than in the middle of the holiday rush.

"Okay," he agreed. "You can let her know we'll be there."

"Thanks for taking one for the team," Nolan quipped.

"Yeah," Heath chuckled, ending the call.

Paris. He was going to Paris. With Julianne. Tomorrow. Even after the happy truce they'd come to, going to Paris together felt like returning to the scene of the crime, somehow. That's where he'd told her he loved her and kissed her for the first time since they were nine years old. They'd left Paris for Spain, and then took a detour to Gibraltar to elope.

With a heavy sigh, Heath got up from the kitchen table and tapped gently at the door to Julianne's studio. Now he had to convince her to go with him. And not just to go, but to go and act like the happy wife *in public*, one of the barriers they hadn't breached. To fool Madame Badeau, they had to be convincing, authentic. That meant his skittish bride would have to tolerate French levels of public affection. It might not even be possible.

The room was silent. She wasn't using her pottery wheel, but he knew she was in there.

"Come in."

Heath twisted the knob and pushed his way into her work space. Julianne was hovering over a sculpture on her table. This was an art piece for her gallery show, he was pretty certain. It was no simple vase, but an intricately detailed figure of a woman dancing.

Julianne's hair was pulled back into a knot. She was wearing a pair of jeans and a fitted T-shirt. There was clay smeared on her shirt, her pants, her face, her arms—she got into her work. It reminded him of that first night they'd spent together, sending a poorly timed surge of desire through him.

"I have a proposition for you, Jules."

At that, Julianne frowned and set down her sculpting tool. "That sound ominous," she noted.

"It depends on how you look at it. I need to take a trip for work. And it's a long story, but I need you to come with me. Do you have a current passport?"

Julianne's eyebrows lifted in surprise. "Yes. I renewed last year, although I haven't gone anywhere. Where on earth do you have to go for work?"

"We're going to Paris this weekend."

"Excuse me?"

Heath held up his hands defensively. "I know. I don't have a choice. It's an important account and the client will only work with me. She's a little temperamental. I know it sounds strange, and I hate to impose, but I have to take you to Paris with me. For, uh…public companionship."

A smile curled Julianne's lips. "I take it the French lady has the hots for you?"

He shook his head in dismay. "Yes, she does. I had to tell her I was married so she'd back off."

"She knows we're married?" Julianne stiffened slightly.

"I had to tell her something. Rebuffing her without good reason might've cost us a critical account. I had to tell my business partner, too, so he was on the same page."

Julianne nodded slowly, processing the information. She obviously didn't care for anyone outside of the two of them and their lawyers knowing about this. It was one thing for family to find out, but who cared if a woman halfway across the globe knew?

"She's insisting I come to Paris to correct some things she's unhappy with and to bring you with me on the trip. I think she wants to meet you, more than anything. It would look suspicious if I didn't bring you. We're supposed to be happily married."

"What does that mean when we get there?"

Heath swallowed hard. They'd gotten to the sticking point. "Exactly what you think it means. We have to publically act like a married couple. We need to wear our rings, be affectionate and do everything we can to convince my client of our rock-solid romance."

Heath looked down and noticed that Julianne was tightly clutching her sculpting tool with white-knuckled strength. "No one here will find out," he added.

Finally, Julianne nodded, dropping the tool and stretching her fingers. "I haven't seen you look this uncomfortable since Sheriff Duke rolled onto the property." She laughed nervously and rubbed her hands clean on her pants.

He doubted he had looked as concerned as she did now. "I can probably get Wade to step in and help while we're gone. Things are in pretty good shape around here. So can I interest you in an all-expense-paid weekend in Paris? We leave tomorrow. My personal discomfort will simply be a bonus."

Julianne nodded and came out from behind her work table. "I get to be a witness to your personal discomfort *and* experience Paris for free? Hmm…I think I can stand being in love with you for a few days for that. But," she added, holding up her hand, "just to be clear, this is all for show to protect your business. Nothing we say or do can be considered evidence of long-suppressed feelings for one another. By the time we get home, the clock will be up on the two of us. Consider this trip our last hoorah."

Nine

"Did you remember to bring your wedding ring?"

Julianne paused in the lobby of J'Adore and started searching in her purse. "I brought it. I just forgot to put it on. What about you?"

Heath held up his left hand and wiggled his fingers. "Got it."

Julianne finally located the small velvet box that held her wedding band. The poor, ignored gold band had been rotting in her jewelry box since the day they returned from their trip to Europe. They'd bought the bands from a small jewelry shop in Gibraltar. With a reputation for being the Las Vegas of Europe, there were quite a few places with wedding bands for last-minute nuptials. They hadn't been very expensive. They were probably little more than nickel painted over with gold-colored paint. Had they been worn for more than a week, the gold might have chipped off long ago, but as it was, they were as perfect and shiny as the day they'd bought them.

She slipped the band onto her finger and put the box away. It felt weird to wear her ring again, especially so close to the finalization of their divorce. Part of her couldn't help thinking this ruse was a mistake. It felt like playing with fire. She'd been burned too many times in her life already.

"Okay, are you ready? This is our first public outing as a married couple. Try to remember not to pull away from me the way you always do."

Julianne winced at his observation. She *did* pull away from him. Even now. Even with no one here having the slightest clue who they were. It was her reflex to shy away from everyone who touched her, at least at first. He seemed to think it was just him instead of a lingering side effect of her attack. She just didn't care to be touched very much. She wanted to tell him that it wasn't about him, but now was not the time to open that can of worms. "I'll do my best," she said instead. "Try not to sneak up on me, though."

Heath nodded and took her hand. "Let's go and get this over with."

They checked in at the front desk and were escorted to the executive offices by Marie, Madame Badeau's personal assistant. The walls and floors were all painted a delicate shade of pink that Heath told her was called "blush" after the company's first cheek color. When they reached the suite outside Madame Badeau's offices, the blush faded to white. White marble floors, white walls, white leather furniture, white lamps and glass and crystal fixtures to accent them.

"*Bonjour,* Monsieur Langston!"

A woman emerged from a frosted pair of double doors. Like the office, she was dressed in an all-white pantsuit. It was tailored to perfection, showing every flawless curve of the older woman's physique. This was no ordinary woman approaching her sixties. There wasn't a single gray hair in her dark brown coiffure. Not a wrinkle, a blemish, or a bit of makeup out of place. This woman had the money to pay the personal trainers and plastic surgeons necessary to preserve her at a solid forty-year-old appearance.

Heath reluctantly let go of Julianne's hand to embrace Madame Badeau and give her kisses on each cheek. "You're looking ravishing, as always, Cecilia."

"You charmer." The woman beamed at Heath, holding his face in her hands. She muttered something in French, but Julianne hadn't a clue what she said.

And then the dark gaze fell on her. "And this must be Madame Langston! Julianne, *oui?*"

At first, Julianne was a little startled by the use of the married name she'd never taken. She recovered quickly by nodding as the woman approached her. She followed Heath's lead in greeting the woman. "Yes. Thank you for allowing me to join Heath on this trip. We haven't been back to Paris since he confessed his love for me at the base of the Eiffel Tower."

Cecilia placed a hand over her heart and sighed. "Such a beautiful moment, I'm sure. You must have dinner there tonight!" The woman's accent made every word sound so lovely, Julianne would've agreed to anything she said. "I will have Marie arrange it."

"That isn't necessary, Cecilia. I'm here to work on the spring J'Adore campaign. Besides, it would be impossible to get reservations on such short notice."

Cecilia puckered her perfectly plumped and painted lips with a touch of irritation. "You are in Paris, Heath. You *must* enjoy yourself. In Paris we do not work twenty-four hours a day. There must be time for wine and conversation. A stroll along the Seine. If you do not make time for that, why even bother to be in Paris at all? *Non*," she said, dismissing his complaint with the elegant wave of her hand. "You will dine there tonight. I am good friends with the owner. Alain will make certain you are accommodated. Is eight o'clock too early?"

Julianne remembered how late Parisian evenings tended to go. Eating dinner at five in the evening was preposterous to them. "That would be lovely," she responded, before Heath could argue again. The last time she was in Paris, they couldn't even afford the ticket to the top, much less dining in their gourmet French restaurant. She would take advantage of it this time, for certain. "*Merci, madame*," she said, using two of the five French words she knew.

Cecilia waved off Marie to make the arrangements. "Quickly, business, then more pleasure," she said with a spark of mischief in her dark eyes. "Heath, your art director has made the arrangement for a second photo shoot today. It should only take a few hours. While we are there, perhaps your *belle femme* would enjoy a luxurious afternoon in the spa downstairs?"

Julianne was about to protest, but the wide smile on Heath's face stopped her before she could speak. "That's a wonderful idea," Heath said. "Jules, the J'Adore spa is a world-famous experience. While I work this out, you can enjoy a few hours getting pampered and ready for dinner this evening. How does that sound?"

She thought for certain that Heath wouldn't want to be left alone with Cecilia, but this didn't seem to bother him at all. Perhaps her appearance had already made all the difference. "*Très bien*," Julianne said with a smile.

Cecilia picked up the phone to make the arrangements and she and Heath settled at her desk to work on some details. Julianne sat quietly, sipping sparkling water and taking in the finer details of the office. A few minutes later, Marie reappeared to escort her to the spa.

Remembering her role as happy wife, Julianne returned to Heath's side and leaned in to give him a passionate, but appropriate kiss. She didn't want to overdo it. The moment their lips met, the ravenous hunger for Heath she'd become all too familiar with returned. She had to force herself to pull away.

"I'm off to be pampered," she said with a smile to cover the flush of arousal as one of excitement. "I'll see you this evening. *Au revoir*," she said, slipping out of the office in Marie's wake.

They returned to the first floor of the building, where a private entrance led them to the facility most customers entered from the street to the right of the J'Adore offices. Marie handed her over to Jacqueline, the manager of the spa.

"Madame Langston, are you ready for your day of pampering?" she said with a polite, subdued smile.

"I am. What am I having done?"

Jacqueline furrowed her brow at her for a moment in confusion, and then she laughed. "Madame Badeau said you are to be given all our finest and most luxurious treatments. You're doing *everything, madame*."

Heath hoped everything went okay with Julianne. Had he not sent her to one of the finest day spas in the world, he might have been worried about working and leaving her alone like that. He'd thought perhaps that he would need her to stay with him all the time, but the moment Cecilia laid eyes on Julianne, the energy she projected toward him shifted. He knew instantly that she would no longer be in pursuit of him, although he wasn't entirely sure what had made the difference.

It wasn't until they were going over the proofs of the photo shoot several hours later that she leaned into him and said, "You love your Julianne very much, I can tell."

At first, he wanted to scoff at her observation, but he realized that he couldn't. Of course he would love his wife. That's how marriages worked. He tried to summon the feelings he'd had for her all those years ago so his words rang with an authenticity Cecilia would recognize. "She was the first and maybe the last woman I'll ever love. The day she said she would marry me was the happiest and scariest day of my life."

That was true enough.

"I see something between you two. I do not see it often. You have something rare and precious. You must treat your love like the most valuable thing you will ever own. Don't ever let it get away from you. You will regret it your entire life, I assure you."

There was a distance in Cecilia's eyes when she spoke that convinced Heath she knew firsthand about that kind of loss. But he couldn't see what she thought she saw in his relationship with Julianne. There might be passion. There might be a nostalgia for the past they shared. But they didn't have the kind of great love Cecilia claimed. A love like that would have survived all these years, shining like a bright star instead of hiding in the shadows like an embarrassing secret. Perhaps they were just better actors than he gave them credit for.

The conversation had ended and they'd finished their day at work. Julianne had texted him to let him know a car was taking her back to their hotel and she would meet him there to go for dinner. Cecilia had booked them a room at the Four Seasons Hotel George V Paris, just off the Chámps Élysées. He arrived there around nightfall, when the town had just begun to famously sparkle and glow.

Perhaps they could walk to the Eiffel Tower. It wasn't a long walk, just a nice stroll across the bridge and along the Seine. The weather was perfect—cool, but not too cold.

He opened the door of their hotel room, barging inside. He found Julianne sitting on the edge of their king-sized bed, fastening the buckle on the ankle strap of her beige heels. His gaze traveled up the length of her bare leg to the nude-colored lace sheath dress she was wearing. It hugged her every curve, giving almost the illusion that she was naked, it so closely matched the creamy ivory of her skin.

Julianne stood up, giving him a better view of the dress. She made a slow turn, showcasing the curve of her backside and the hard muscles of her calves in those sky-high nude pumps with red soles. The peek of red was the only pop of color aside from the matching red painted on her lips. "What do you think?"

"It's…" he began, but his mouth was so dry he had difficulty forming the words. "Very nice."

"When I got done a little early, I decided to go shopping. It's a Dolce & Gabbana dress. And these are Christian Louboutin shoes. I honestly can't believe I spent as much money as I did, but after all that pampering, I was feeling indulgent and carefree for once."

"It's worth every penny," Heath said. In that moment he wanted to buy her a hundred dresses if they would make her beam as radiantly as she did right now. "But now I'm underdressed. Give me a few minutes and I'll be ready to go."

Heath didn't have a tuxedo with him, but he pulled out his finest black Armani suit and the ivory silk dress shirt that would perfectly match her dress. He showered quickly to rinse away the grit and worries of the day and changed into the outfit.

"I was going to suggest we walk since it's so nice, but I'm thinking those shoes aren't meant for city strolls."

"Even if they were, Marie arranged for a car to pick us up at seven forty-five. Perhaps we can walk home." Julianne gathered up a small gold clutch and pulled a gold wrap around her shoulders.

Heath held out his arm to usher her out the door. In the lobby, a driver was waiting for them. He led them outside to the shiny black Bentley. They relaxed in the soft leather seats as the driver carried them through the dark streets and across the bridge to the left bank where the Eiffel Tower stood.

The driver escorted them to the entrance reserved for guests of the Jules Verne restaurant. The private elevator whisked them to the second floor in moments. Heath remembered climbing the over six hundred stairs to reach this floor eleven years ago. The lift entrance tickets were double the price, so they'd skipped it and walked up. The elevator was decidedly more luxurious and didn't make his thighs quiver.

They were seated at a table for two right against the glass overlooking Paris. Out the window, they could see the numerous bridges stretching over the Seine and the glowing, vaulted glass ceiling of the Grand Palais beyond it. The view was breathtaking. Romantic. It made him wish he'd been able to afford a place like this when they were kids. Proposing from the lawn had been nice, but not nice enough for their relationship to last. Caviar and crème fraîche might not a good marriage make, but it couldn't have hurt.

They both ordered wine and the tasting menu of the evening. Then they sat nervously fidgeting with their napkins and looking out the window for a few minutes. Pretending to be a couple in front of Cecilia was one thing. Now they were smack-dab in the middle of one of the most romantic places on earth with no one to make a show for.

They'd spent the last few weeks together. They shared a bed nearly every night. But they hadn't done any of that in Paris, the city where they fell in love. Paris was the wild card that scared Heath to death. He'd done a good job to keep his distance in all of this. Julianne's remoteness made that easier. He liked to think that in a few short days, he would be divorced and happy about that fact.

But Paris could change everything. It had once; it could do it again. The question was whether or not he wanted it to. He shouldn't. It was the same self-destructive spiral that had kept him in this marriage for eleven long years. But that didn't keep him from wanting the thing he'd been promised the day they married.

As the first course arrived, he opted to focus on his food instead of the way the warm lighting made her skin look like soft velvet. He wouldn't pay attention to the way she closed her eyes and savored each bite that passed her lips. And he certainly would ignore the way she occasionally glanced at him when she thought he wasn't looking.

That was just asking for trouble and he had his hands full already.

"We have to stay and watch the lights."

Julianne led Heath out from beneath the Eiffel Tower to the long stretch of dark lawn that sprawled beside it. The first time they had been here, they'd laid out on a blanket. Tonight, they weren't prepared and there was no way she would tempt the fabric of her new dress with grass stains, so she stopped at one of the gravel paths that dissected the lawn.

"We've seen them before, Jules."

She frowned at him, ignoring his protests. They were

watching the lights. "It's five minutes out of your busy life, Heath. Relax. The moment it's over, we'll head back to the hotel, okay?"

With a sigh, he stopped protesting and took his place beside her. It wasn't long before the tower went dark and the spectacular dance of sparkling lights lit up the steel structure. It twinkled like something out of a fairy tale. Heath put his arm around her shoulder and she slipped into the nook of his arm, sighing with contentment.

Heath might be uncomfortable here because this was where their relationship had changed permanently, but Julianne was happy to be back. This had been the moment where she was the happiest. The moment she'd allowed herself to really love Heath for the first time. She'd been fighting the feelings for months. Once he said he loved her, there was no more holding back. It had been one of those beautiful moments, as if they'd been in a movie, where everything is perfect and romantic.

It was later that everything went wrong.

The lights finally stopped and the high beams returned to illuminate the golden goddess from the base. Julianne turned and found Heath looking at her instead of the tower. There was something in his eyes in that moment that she couldn't quite put her finger on. She knew what she wanted to see. What she wanted to happen. If this *had* been a movie, Heath would have taken her into his arms and kissed her with every ounce of passion in his body. Then he would have said he loved her and that he didn't want a divorce.

But this was real life. Instead, the light in his eyes faded. He politely offered her his arm and they turned and continued down the path to the sidewalk that would lead them back to the Seine. Julianne swallowed her disappointment and tried to focus on the positives of the evening instead of the fantasy she'd built in her head.

As they neared the river, the cool night air off the water made Julianne shiver. The gold wrap was more decorative than functional.

"Here," Heath said, slipping out of his coat and holding it for her. "Put this on."

"Thank you," Julianne replied, accepting the jacket. "It's quite a bit cooler than it was when we went to dinner." She snuggled into the warm, soft fabric, the scent of Heath's skin and cologne comingling in the air surrounding her. It instantly brought to mind the hot nights they'd spent together over the last few weeks. The familiar need curled in her belly, urging her to reach for him and tell him to take her back to the hotel so she could make love to him.

Despite the night chill, her cheeks flooded with warmth. She no longer needed the coat, but she kept it on anyway. As much as she craved his touch, she wasn't in a hurry to end this night. The sky was clear and sparkling with a sprinkle of stars. The moon hung high and full overhead. After the emotionally trying few weeks they'd had, they were sharing a night together in Paris. She wouldn't rush that even to make love to Heath.

They stopped on the bridge and looked out at the moon reflecting on the water. It was such a calm, clear night, the water was like glass. In the distance, she could hear street performers playing jazz music. Heath was beside her. For the first time in a long time, Julianne felt a sense of peace. Here, there were no detectives asking questions, no family to accommodate, no unfinished art projects haunting her and no dead men chasing her in her dreams. It was just the two of them in the most romantic city in the world.

"Do you remember when we put the lock on the Pont des Arts bridge?"

Heath nodded. The bridge was farther down the Seine near the Louvre. It was covered in padlocks that had couples' names and dates written on them. Some couples came on their wedding day with special engraved locks. Others bought them from street vendors on the spur of the moment, like they had. The man had loaned them a marker to write "Heath and Julianne Forever." They'd put the lock on the bridge and threw the key into the river before heading to the train station and leaving Paris for Spain. The idea was that you were sealing your relationship forever. Perhaps that was why she couldn't fully let go of him.

"I wonder if it's still there."

"I doubt it," he said. "I read that they cut locks off or remove entire panels of the fence at night. It's been eleven years. I'm sure our lock is long gone."

Julianne frowned at the water. That wasn't the answer she was looking for. A part of her was thinking they would be able to walk down to the bridge and find it. That they might be overcome with emotions at seeing it firmly clasped to the fence, never to be unlocked, and they would finally be able to triumph over the obstacles that were keeping them apart.

Yes, because that's exactly what she needed to do when her divorce was virtually finalized. But if she were honest with herself, if she let her tightly clamped down emotions free like she did that night in Paris all those years ago, she had to admit nothing had changed. She still loved Heath. She had always loved him. It was her love for him that had forced her to push him away so he could have a real chance at happiness. And it was her love for him that wouldn't let her cut the cord that tied them together. She didn't need a lock to do that.

Heath had accused her of commitment-phobia, of using their marriage to keep men away. But that wasn't the whole truth. The whole truth was that she could never love any of those men. How could she? Her heart belonged to Heath and had since elementary school.

"That makes me sad," she admitted to the dark silence around them. "I was hoping that somehow our lock would last even though we didn't. Our love should still be alive here in Paris, just like it was then."

Heath reached for her hand and held it tight. He didn't say anything, but he didn't have to. The warm comfort of his touch was enough. She didn't expect him to feel the same way. She'd thrown his feelings back in his face and never told him why. He'd asked for a divorce, so despite their mutual attraction and physical indulgence over the last few weeks, that was all he felt for her. He'd carried the torch for her far longer than he should have, so she couldn't begrudge him finally putting it down. Telling Heath she had feelings for him *now*, after all this time, would be like rubbing salt in the wound.

Instead of focusing on that thought, she closed her eyes and enjoyed the feel of Heath's touch. In a few weeks, even that would be gone. Carrying on their physical relationship after the divorce wasn't a good idea. They were divorcing so Heath could move on with his life. Find a woman who could love him the way he deserved to be loved. Maybe take his mystery woman to the Caribbean. For that to happen, she couldn't keep stringing him along. She had to let him go.

She needed to make the most of the time they had left and indulge her heart's desires. And tonight, she intended to indulge in the fancy, king-sized bed of their hotel suite. She wanted the passionate, romantic night in Paris that she couldn't have when they were young and in love.

Julianne opened her eyes and turned to look at Heath. His gaze met hers, a similar sadness there although he hadn't voiced it. He probably thought they were mourning their marriage together in the place where it started. That was the smart thing for her to do. To appreciate what they had and to let it go once and for all.

She pressed her body to his side and with the help of her stilettos, easily tilted her head up to whisper into his ear. "Take me home."

Ten

Heath opened the door to their suite and Julianne stepped inside ahead of him. In a bucket by the seating area was a bottle of Champagne with a note. Julianne plucked the white card from the bottle and scanned the neat script.

"Madame Badeau has sent us a bottle of Champagne. She's not quite the cougar you warned me about, Heath."

Heath was slipping out of his coat jacket and tugging at his tie when he turned to look at her. "She told me earlier tonight that she could see we had a rare and precious love."

Julianne's eyes widened at him, but he didn't notice. He was too busy chuckling and shaking his head.

"Boy, did we have her fooled. I think she's finally given up on me."

She swallowed the lump in her throat and cast the card onto the table. A woman she'd known less than a day could see what Heath refused to see. "Spoils to the victor," she replied, trying to keep the bitter tone from her voice. "Open it while I change."

He walked over to take the bottle from her. When she heard the loud pop of the cork, she moved the two crystal flutes closer to him and took a few steps away to watch as he poured.

As many times as they had been together over the last few weeks, there hadn't been much fanfare to their love-making. No seduction. No temptation. It hadn't been as frantic as that first night in the shower, but they wanted each other too badly to delay their desires. But tonight she wanted to offer him a night in Europe they'd never forget, this time, for all the right reasons.

Heath set down the bottle and picked up the flutes filled with golden bubbly liquid. His gaze met hers, but instead of approaching him, she smiled softly and let her gold wrap fall to the floor. She reached for the zipper at her side, drawing it down the curve of her waist and swell of her hip. His gaze immediately went to the intimate flash of her skin now exposed and the conspicuous absence of lingerie beneath it.

Julianne knew the exact moment he realized she hadn't been wearing panties all evening. He swallowed hard and his fingers tightened around the delicate crystal stems of the glasses. His chest swelled with a deep breath before his gaze met hers again. There was a hard glint of desire there. He might not love her any longer, but there was no question that he wanted her. The intensity of his gaze stole the breath from her lungs.

Drawing in a much-needed lungful of cool air, she turned her back to Heath and strolled into the bedroom. Her fingertips curled around the hem of her dress, pulling it up and over her head. Her hair spilled back down around her shoulders, tickling her bare shoulder blades. She tossed the dress across the plush chaise and turned around.

Heath had followed her into the bedroom. He stood just

inside the doorway, clutching the glasses in an attempt to keep control. She was surprised he hadn't snapped the delicate stems in half. Julianne stalked across the room toward him, naked except for her gold jewelry and the five-inch heels she was still wearing. She stopped just in front of him. She reached past the glasses to the button of his collar. Her nimble fingers made quick work of his shirt, moving down the front until she could part the linen and place her palms on the hard, bare muscles of his chest.

He stood stone still as she worked, his eyes partly closed when she touched him. He reopened them at last when she took one of the glasses from him and held it up for a toast.

"To Paris," she said.

"To Paris," Heath repeated, his voice low and strained. He didn't drink; he just watched Julianne as she put the Champagne to her lips and took a healthy sip.

"Mmm…" she said, her eyes focused only on him. "This is good. I know what would make it better, though."

Leaning into Heath, she held up her flute and poured a stream of the Champagne down his neck. Moving quickly, she lapped at the drops that ran down his throat and pooled in the hollow of his collarbone. She let her tongue drag along his neck, meeting the rough stubble of his five o'clock shadow and feeling the low growl rumbling in his throat.

"You like that?" she asked.

Heath's arm shot out to wrap around her bare waist and tug her body close. Startled, Julianne smacked hard against the wall of his chest, pressing her breasts into him. She could feel the cool moisture of the Champagne on his skin as it molded to hers. When she looked up, he had a wicked grin across his face.

"Oh, yeah," he said. He took a sip of Champagne and then brought his lips to hers. The bubbly liquid filled her own mouth and danced around her tongue before she swallowed it.

Their mouths were still locked onto one another as Heath walked her slowly back toward the bed. With his arm still hooked around the small of her back, he eased Julianne's body down slowly until she met with the cool silky fabric of the duvet.

He pulled away long enough to look longingly at her body and whip off his shirt. Then he poured the rest of the Champagne into the valley between her breasts. He cast the empty flute onto the soft carpet with a thud and dipped his head to clean up the mess he'd made. His tongue slid along her sternum, teasing at the inner curves of her breasts and down to her ribcage. He used his fingertip to dip into her navel and then rub the Champagne he found there over the hardened peaks of her nipples. He bathed them in the expensive alcohol, then took his time removing every drop from her skin.

Julianne arched into his mouth and his hands, urging him on and gasping aloud as he sucked hard at her breast. Her own empty Champagne flute rolled from her hand across the mattress. She brought her hands to his head, burying her fingers in his thick hair and tugging him closer. He resisted her pull, moving lower down her stomach to the dripping golden liquid that waited for him there. His searing lips were like fire across her Champagne-chilled skin. She ached for him to caress every part of her and he happily complied.

Heath's hands pressed against her inner thighs, easing them apart and slipping between them and out of her reach. She had to clutch handfuls of the luxurious linens beneath them to ground herself to the earth as his mouth found her heated core. His tongue worked over her sensitive skin, drawing a chorus of strangled cries from her throat. He was relentless, slipping a finger inside of her until she came undone.

"Heath!" she gasped, her body undulating and pulsing with the pleasure surging through her. She hadn't wanted to find her release without him, not tonight, but he didn't give her the option. She collapsed back against the mattress, her muscles tired and her lungs burning.

She pried open her eyes when she felt the heat of Heath's body moving up over her again. He had shed the last of his clothing, his skin gliding bare along hers.

A moment later, his hazel eyes were staring down into her own. She could feel the firm heat of his desire pressing against her thigh. Eleven years ago this moment had sent her scrambling. The need and nerves in Heath's loving gaze had twisted horribly in her mind to the vicious leer of her attacker. Now there were only the familiar green and gold starbursts of the eyes she fantasized about.

She reached out to him, her palms making contact with the rough stubble of his cheeks. She pulled his mouth to hers and lost herself in him. Instead of fear, there was a peace and comfort in Heath's arms. When he surged forward and filled her aching body with his, she gasped against his mouth but refused to let go. She needed this, needed him.

Julianne drew her legs up, cradling his hips and drawing him deeper inside. She wanted to get as close to him as she could. To take in Heath and keep a part of him there inside her forever. The clock was ticking on their time together, but she could have this.

As the pace increased, Heath finally had to tear away from her lips. He buried his face in her neck, his breath hot and ragged as he thrust hard and fast. Her body, which had been exhausted mere moments ago, was alive and tingling with sensation once again. Her release built inside, her muscles tightening and straining like a taut rubber band as she got closer and closer. Heath's body was equally tense beneath her fingertips, a sheen of perspiration forming on his skin.

"I've never…wanted a woman…as much as I want you, Julianne."

His words were barely a whisper in her ear amongst the rough gasps and rustling sheets, but she heard them and felt them to her innermost core. Her heart stuttered in her chest. It wasn't a declaration of love, but it was serious. She couldn't remember the last time he'd used her full name when he spoke to her. And then it hit her and she knew why his words impacted her so greatly. When he'd said their wedding vows.

I take thee, Julianne Renee Eden, to be my lawfully wedded wife from this day forward.

The words from the past echoed in her mind, the image of the boy he was back then looking at her with so much love and devotion in his eyes. No one had ever looked at her like that again. Because no one had ever loved her the way he did. She might have ruined it, but she had his love once and she would cherish that forever.

"Only you," she whispered. "I've only ever wanted you."

There was the slightest hesitation in his movement, and then he thrust inside of her like never before. For a moment, she wondered what that meant, but before she could get very far with her thoughts, her body tugged her out of her own head. The band snapped inside and the rush of pleasure exploded through her. She gasped and cried into his shoulder, clutching him tightly even as he kept surging forward again and again.

"Julianne," he groaned as his whole body shuddered with his own release.

With Heath's face buried in her neck and their hearts beating a rapid tattoo together, she wanted to say the words. It was the right moment to tell him that she loved him. That she wanted to throw their divorce papers out the window and be with him. To confess the truth about what had happened on their wedding night and explain that it wasn't a lack of loving him, but that she was too damaged to give herself to anyone. It had taken years of therapy to get where she was now. She couldn't have expected him to wait for her.

But she knew telling him the whole truth would hurt him more than his imagined insults. All the boys carried a burden of being unable to protect her, but Heath most of all. If Heath knew that the end for Tommy had come too late…that he had already pillaged her thirteen-year-old innocence before he arrived, he would be devastated. Their marriage would no longer be his biggest regret; that moment would replace it and he would be reminded of it every time he looked at her.

Julianne wanted Heath to look at her with desire and passion. She didn't dare ask for love. But if he knew the truth, he would see her as a victim. He would know the full extent of the damage Tommy had caused and that would be all he would see. Could he make love to her without thinking about it?

Julianne squeezed her eyes shut and her mouth with them. She couldn't tell him. She couldn't tell anyone. No matter how much she loved Heath and how badly he deserved to know the truth, the price of voicing the words was too high. She'd rather he believe she was a flighty, spoiled little girl who couldn't decide what she wanted and stomped on his heart like a ripe tomato.

Heath rolled onto his side and wrapped his arm around her waist. He tugged her body against his, curling her into the protective cocoon to keep her warm. Even now, without realizing it, he was trying to protect her. Just like he always had.

Heath could never ever know that he'd failed that day.

The drive back to Cornwall from Hartford was long and quiet. Heath wasn't entirely sure what was going on with Julianne, but she'd barely spoken a word since they'd departed Paris earlier that morning. How was it that their relationship didn't seem to work on U.S. soil?

They pulled up at the bunkhouse and stumbled inside with their bags. It had been a long day, even traveling by private jet. The sun was still up but it was late into the night on Parisian time.

Heath was pulling the door shut behind him when he nearly slammed into Julianne's back. She had stopped short, her bags still in her arms, her gaze fixed firmly on the kitchen table.

"What is it?" he asked, leaning to one side to look around her. She didn't answer, but she didn't have to. Molly had brought in an overnighted package and left it on the table for them. The same type of packaging the divorce papers had originally arrived in. That only brought one option to mind. The thirty-day waiting period was up. A judge had signed the papers and her lawyer had mailed them.

They were divorced.

Just like that. After eleven years, their relationship was possibly better than it had ever been and they were divorced. Heath took a deep breath and closed his eyes. He wanted this. He had asked for this. He'd harassed her and demanded his freedom. And now he had what he wanted and he'd never felt so frustrated in his life.

He unceremoniously dropped his bags to the floor and

walked around Julianne to pick up the envelope. It had her name on it, but he opened it anyway. There was probably a similar envelope being held at the front desk of his building, waiting for him to return to Manhattan.

A quick glance inside confirmed his suspicions. With a sad nod, he dropped the papers back to the table. "Welcome home," he said with a dry tone.

"The time went by quickly, didn't it?"

He looked up, surprised at her first words in quite a while. "Time flies when you're having fun."

Julianne's eyes narrowed at him, her lips tightening as she nodded. She didn't look like she was having fun. She also didn't look pleased with him although he had no clue what the problem was.

"Julianne…" he began, but she held up her hand to silence him.

"Don't, Heath. This is what we wanted. I know the last few weeks have muddied the water between us, but it doesn't change the fact that we shouldn't be married. We aren't meant to be together long-term. As you said, we were having fun. But fun is all it was, right?"

Heath swallowed the lump in his throat. That was his intention, but it had started to feel like more. At some point, he had forgotten about the divorce and just focused on being with her. Was he the only one that felt that way? It didn't seem like it at the time. It seemed like she had gotten invested as well. Perhaps that was just Paris weaving its magic spell on their relationship again. "Fun," he muttered.

Julianne brushed past him and pulled her wedding ring off her finger. They were both still wearing them after their weekend charade for Madame Badeau. She placed it on top of the paperwork. "We won't need these anymore."

Even as she said the words, Heath got the feeling that

she didn't mean them. She was unhappy. Her, the girl who slammed the door in his face and told him to move on. When he finally tries, she takes it personally.

"So now what?" he asked. Heath wasn't sure how to proceed from here. Did getting a divorce mean their fling was over? They still had the crush of the Christmas season ahead of them. He wasn't looking forward to the long, cold nights in bed without her.

"I think it's time for me to move back into the big house," she said, although she wouldn't look him in the eye.

"Why?"

"When I spoke with Mom yesterday, she said the live-in nurse would be leaving tomorrow. They were able to move Dad's bed back upstairs since he's getting around well. That means I can have my room back."

"Your studio is out here."

She nodded. "But under the circumstances, I think it might be better if we put some distance between us."

Heath's hands balled into angry fists at his side. It was his idea to move forward with the divorce and yet it still felt like Julianne was breaking up with him all over again. "Why is it that whenever our relationship gets even remotely serious, you run away?"

Her eyes met his, a flash of green anger lighting them. "Run away? I'm not running away. There's nothing to run from, Heath. As I understand it, we were just having some fun and passing the time. I don't know if that qualifies as a relationship."

She was lying. He knew she was lying. She had feelings for him, but she was holding them back. Nothing had changed with her in all these years. She loved him then, just as she loved him now, but she refused to admit it. She always pulled away when it mattered. Yeah, he hadn't confessed that he had developed feelings for her, but what fool would? He'd done it once and got burned pretty badly.

"Why do I get the feeling that you're always lying to me, Jules? Then, now, I never get the whole story."

Her eyes widened. She didn't expect him to call her on it, he could tell. She sputtered a moment before finding her words again. "I-I'm not always lying to you. You know me too well for me to lie."

"You'd think so, and yet you'll look me in the eye and tell me we were just 'having fun.' We've had a lot of sex over the last few weeks, but that's the only barrier I've broken through with you, Jules. You're still keeping secrets."

"You keep your secrets, too, Heath."

"Like what?" he laughed.

"Like the reason why you really wanted a divorce."

Heath had no clue what she was talking about. "And what exactly did I say that was a lie?"

"It may not have been a lie, but you have certainly kept your relationship with that other woman quiet while you were sleeping with me the last few weeks. Now you're free to take her to the Caribbean, right?"

"What woman?"

"The so-called Sweetheart you were gushing at on the phone that day."

"You mean my sixty-three-year-old secretary?" He chuckled, although it wasn't so much out of amusement as annoyance. "I knew you were listening in on my phone call."

"You laid it on pretty thick. Do you really expect me to believe your sweetheart is a woman older than Mom?"

"You should. She likes to be flirted with, so I call her all sorts of pet names. I told her if she held down the fort while I was gone that I would give her a bonus big enough to cover the vacation she wants to take to the beach with her grandkids. Without *me*," he added. "Do you really think I would've pursued something with you while I had a woman on the side?"

Julianne's defiant shoulders slumped a bit at his words. "Then why did you really want the divorce, Heath? You came in here demanding it out of nowhere. I thought for sure you had another woman in mind."

"There's no other woman, Jules. How could there be? I'm not about to get serious with any woman while I'm married to you. That's not fair to her. Just like it wasn't fair to your almost fiancé. You just play with men's minds but you have no intention of ever giving as much as you take. You're right. It's a good thing this was just 'fun' to pass the time. It would be foolish of me to think otherwise and fall for your games twice."

"How dare you!" she said. "You don't know anything about my relationships. You don't know anything about what I've gone through in my life."

"You're right," he said. "Because you won't tell me anything!"

"I have always been as honest as I could be with you, Heath."

"Honest? Really. Then tell me the truth about what happened on our wedding night, Jules. The truth. Not some made-up story about you changing your mind. You were in love with me. You wanted me. The next minute everything changed. Why?"

Julianne stiffened, tears glazing her eyes. Her jaw tightened as though she was fighting to keep the flow of words inside. "Any question but that one," she managed to say.

"That's the only question I want answered. Eleven years I've spent wondering how you could love me one minute and run from me the next. Tell me why. I deserve to know."

Her gaze dropped to the floor. "I can't do that."

"Then you're right, Jules. We shouldn't be married. I'm glad we've finally gotten that matrimonial monkey off our backs. Maybe now I can move on and find a woman who will let me into her life instead of just letting me be a spectator."

"Heath, I—"

"You know," he interrupted, "all I ever wanted from you was for you to let me in. Over the years, I've given you my heart, my soul. I've lied for you. Protected you. I would've gone to jail before I let anyone lay a finger on you. And hell, I still might if Sheriff Duke comes back around. I'd do it gladly. Even now, although I really don't know why. I just don't understand you, Jules. Why do you keep me at arm's length? Even when we're in bed together, you've kept your distance, kept your secrets. Is it me? Or do you treat all men this way?"

Julianne looked back up at him and this time, the tears were flowing freely. It made his chest ache, even as he fought with her, to see her cry that way. But he had to know. Why did she push him away?

"Just you," she said. Then she turned and walked upstairs alone.

Eleven

Julianne sat on the edge of the bed staring at the bags she'd already packed. This morning, she would move back into the big house where she belonged. It broke her heart and made her cry every time she thought about it for too long, but she had to do it. They were divorced. No matter how much she loved him, Heath deserved to be happy. He deserved his freedom and a chance with a woman who could give him everything he wanted.

As much as she wanted to be, Julianne would never be that woman. She would always have her secrets. She would always have a part of herself that she held back from him. Even if she told him it was for his own good, he wouldn't believe her.

After the last few weeks together, she could tell he was confused. It was easy to feel like things were different when they were together so much, but that wouldn't last forever. They'd end up caught in the same circular trap where they'd spent the last eleven years. But she could get them out of it, even if he didn't seem to like it at the time.

He wanted his freedom and she would give it to him.

With a sigh, she stood up and extended the handle of her roller bag. She was nearly to the door of her room when she heard a loud banging at the front door.

She left her luggage behind and went downstairs. The low rumble of male voices turned into distinguishable words as she reached the landing.

"I'm going to have to bring her in for questioning."

"Why? You've asked a million questions. What do you want with her?"

Sheriff Duke was lurking in the door frame, looking larger and more threatening than ever before. "I need to talk to her. We also need a hair sample."

Heath glanced over his shoulder to see Julianne standing at the foot of the stairs. He cursed silently and turned back to the doorway. "Ask her your questions here. And get a warrant for the hair. Otherwise, you have to arrest us both."

"I can't arrest you just because you ask me to, Heath."

"Fine. Then arrest me because I killed Tommy."

Duke's eyes widened for a moment, but he didn't hesitate to reach for his handcuffs. "All right. Heath Langston, you're under arrest for the murder of Thomas Wilder. You have the right…"

The sheriff's voice faded out as the reality of what was happening hit her. Sixteen years' worth of karma was about to fly back in their faces. And to make things worse, Heath had confessed. Why had he confessed?

Duke clamped the cuffs on Heath's wrists and walked him to the back of the squad car.

"Don't say anything, Jules," she heard Heath say before the door slammed shut.

Returning to face Julianne, Duke started his speech again and reached for his second pair of cuffs. She stood silent and still, letting him close the cold metal shackles around her wrists. He took her to the other side of the squad car and sat her there beside Heath.

The ride into town was deadly silent. Anything they said could be used against them, after all. It wasn't until they were led into separate interrogation rooms that the nervous flutter of her stomach started up.

An hour went by. Then two.

She didn't have her watch on, but she was fairly certain that nearly four hours had passed before Sheriff Duke finally came in clutching a file of paperwork. Her stomach was starting to growl, which meant lunchtime had come and gone.

He settled down at the table across from her. No one else was in the room, but she had no idea how many people were gathered on the other side of the one-way glass panel. He flipped through his pages, clicked the button on his pen and looked up at her.

"Heath had a lot to say, Julianne."

She took a deep breath. "About what?" she replied as innocently as she could.

"About killing Tommy."

"I'm not sure why he would say something like that."

"I'm not sure, either. He had a pretty detailed story. If I didn't know better I'd lock him up right now and be done with it."

"Why don't you?"

A smirk crossed the policeman's face and Julianne didn't care for it. He was too pleased, as though he had everything figured out. He was probably already planning to use this big case to bolster his reelection.

"Well, as good a tale as he told me, it just doesn't match

up with the evidence. You see, Heath told me that he found Tommy on top of you and he hit him on the back of his head with a rock to stop him, accidentally killing him."

Julianne didn't blink, didn't breathe, didn't so much as shift her gaze in one direction or another.

"Problem is that the coroner says Tommy was killed instantly by a blow to his left temple."

"I thought they said on the news that Tommy had the back of his head bashed in." She tried to remember what she had seen on television. That's what the reports had said. Only she knew that injury came second. She didn't know if he was already dead by then or not.

"He did. But we don't release all the critical information to the news. Like the hair we found."

"Hair?" She hadn't heard anything about hair, either.

"You'd think that after all these years that any evidence would be destroyed, and most of it was, but we were lucky. Tommy died with a few strands of long blond hair snagged on the ring he was wearing. Hair and bone are usually all that's left after this length of time. It was as though he'd had a handful of a woman's hair in his hand shortly before he died."

"There are a lot of blondes in Cornwall."

"That's true, but Heath has already stated he saw Tommy on top of you, so that's narrowing it down for me."

"You said you didn't believe his story."

"I said it didn't match the coroner's report. And it doesn't. So that made me think perhaps he was protecting you. That made a lot of the pieces click together in my mind. Why don't you just save me the trouble and tell me the truth, Julianne. You don't really want me to charge Heath with Tommy's murder do you?"

"It wouldn't be murder," she argued. "It would be self-defense."

"Not exactly. He wasn't being threatened, just you. It might have been accidental, but his lawyers will need to prove it. There's nothing that says he didn't come up on Tommy in the woods and bludgeon him for no reason."

Julianne swallowed the lump in her throat. She wouldn't let Heath take the blame for this. She just couldn't. He'd always told her it wouldn't come to this, but if it did, he wouldn't be charged because he was protecting her. The sadistic gleam in Sheriff Duke's eyes made her think Heath might be wrong about that. Heath wouldn't spend a single day in jail protecting her. This had all gone on far too long. Keeping him out of prison was far more important than protecting his ego.

"I'm the one that killed Tommy. He…" She fought for the words she'd only said aloud a few times in her therapist's office. "He raped me," she spat out.

Sheriff Duke's eyes widened for a moment and he sat back into his chair. He didn't speak, but he reached over to check his voice recorder to make sure it caught everything.

She took a moment trying to decide where to go from there. "I was doing my chores after school. Same as any other day. The next thing I knew, Tommy was there, watching me. I was startled at first, but I thought I would be okay. Until he pulled out a switchblade and started walking toward me. I ran, but he grabbed my ponytail and yanked me back. I fell onto the ground and he was on top of me in an instant.

"He was so large. Bigger than my brothers. I was only thirteen and smaller than other girls my age. There was no way to fight him off. He had the knife at my throat so I couldn't scream. I kicked and fought at first, but he grabbed a fistful of my hair and yanked hard enough to bring tears to my eyes. He said if I didn't keep still, he'd cut my throat and leave my body naked for my daddy to find me."

Julianne's hands started trembling. The metal of the handcuffs tapped against the tabletop, so she pulled her arms back to rest in her lap. Her eyes focused on the table instead of the man watching her.

"I knew in the pit of my stomach that I was dead. No matter what he said, he wasn't going to let me run to my parents or the police. He would finish this and me before he was done. I tried to keep my focus and ignore the pain. It would've been so easy to tune everything out, but I knew that I couldn't. I knew that eventually, he'd get distracted and I would have my one and only chance to escape.

"I was able to slowly feel along the ground beside me. At first, there was nothing but pea gravel. I could've thrown that in his eyes, but it would have only made him angry. Then I found a rock. It was small but dense with a sharp edge I could feel with my fingertips. He still had the knife at my throat and if it wasn't enough to knock him out, I knew it was all over, but I didn't care. I had to do it. I brought the rock up and slammed it into the side of his head as hard as I could."

Julianne had seen this image in her dreams a thousand times so it was easy to describe even after all this time. "His eyes rolled into his head and he collapsed onto me. I struggled as quickly as I could to push him up and off of me. When I was finally able to shove him off, his head flung back and struck a rock sticking up out of the ground. That's when he started bleeding. I panicked. I kicked the knife away from him and started pulling my clothes back on. That's when Heath found me.

"We kept waiting for Tommy to get up, but he didn't. That's when we realized that hitting his head on the rock must have killed him. There was so much blood on the ground. He told me to sit tight while he went for help. He came back with the other boys. The rest was a blur, but I heard him tell the others that he'd hit Tommy with the rock when he saw him attacking me. There were so many times that we should've stopped and gone to the house to call the police, but we were so scared. In the end, all they wanted to do was protect me. And they did. None of them deserve to get in trouble for that."

"What about the note Tommy left? And all his things that were missing?"

"We did that," she said, not mentioning one brother or another specifically. "We were running on adrenaline, reacting faster than we could think. We hid the body, destroyed all his stuff and tried to pretend like it never happened."

"That didn't exactly work out for you, did it?"

Julianne looked up at the sheriff. He didn't seem even remotely moved by her story. He tasted blood and no matter what she said, she was certain he wasn't going to just close the case based on her testimony. "It's hard to pretend you haven't been raped, Sheriff Duke."

"And yet you waited all these years to come forward. It seems to me like you're hiding something. I think—"

A loud rap on the one-way glass interrupted him. Duke's jaw tightened and he closed the folder with his paperwork. "I'll be back," he said. He got up and left the room.

Julianne wasn't certain what had happened, but she was relieved for the break. It took a lot out of her to tell that story. Whether or not he backed down and dismissed the charges as self-defense, she knew she would have to tell that story again. And again. A part of her was terrified, but another part of her felt liberated. This secret had been like a concrete block tied around her neck. She knew it had to feel the same way to the others.

Maybe, finally, they could all stop living with the dark cloud of Tommy's death over their heads.

They sure were slow to book him. Heath had spent hours waiting for the inevitable. He'd told them he killed Tommy. Certainly the wheels of progress should be turning by now.

Not long after that, the door opened and Sheriff Duke's deputy, Jim, came through the door. "You can go."

"What?" He stood up from his chair. "I can go?"

Jim came over and unlocked the handcuffs. "Yes." He opened the door and held it.

Heath was thoroughly confused, but he wasn't about to wait for them to change their minds. In the hallway, he found several people waiting there. He recognized the woman as Tommy Wilder's sister, Deborah Curtis. Brody had sent them all the background report on her when she came to Cornwall asking about her brother. She was standing there with a man wearing an expensive tailored suit. He carried himself like he was important somehow, like he was her lawyer. Heath froze on the spot. Was she here to confront him for killing her brother?

Another door opened off the hallway and Julianne stepped out with a disgusted-looking Sheriff Duke at her side.

"What is going on?" Heath asked.

Julianne shook her head. "I have no clue. Duke said I was free to go."

The man beside Deborah stepped forward. "My name is Pat Richards. I'm a prosecutor for the state of Connecticut. With the evidence I have, your testimony and that of Mrs. Curtis, the state has opted not to press charges. This situation was tragic, but obviously in self-defense. I can't in good conscience prosecute Julianne after everything she went through."

Heath frowned. "Prosecute Julianne? I'm the one that confessed to killing him."

Pat smiled wide and nodded in understanding. "A noble thing, for sure, but it wasn't necessary. The charges have been dropped. You're both free to go."

Sheriff Duke shook his head and disappeared down the hallway into his office with a slam of his door.

"He disagrees, I take it?"

The prosecutor chuckled. "He fancied himself the hero cracking a huge case. There's not much crime around here for him to tackle, and this would give him the boost for his reelection. But even without Mrs. Curtis's testimony of her own attack, there was nothing for us to go forward on."

"What?" This time the question came from Julianne.

Deborah stepped forward, speaking for the first time. "I want you to know that I don't harbor any ill will against you or your family. You took Tommy in when no one else would and did only what you had to do to defend yourself. I completely understand that. My brother started displaying violent tendencies before he was even twelve years old. My parents tried to control him. They punished him, they put him in therapy. They even considered one of the boot camps for troubled teens. But it wasn't until my father came home early from work one day and caught him... attacking me..."

Julianne gasped, bringing her hand to cover her mouth. "Oh, god." Heath wanted to go to her side, but he resisted. Despite what had happened, she might still be upset with him.

"Tommy didn't succeed," Deborah said, "but he would've raped me if my father hadn't come home. I didn't want to press charges, I was too embarrassed. After that, he wasn't allowed to be alone with me. His close call didn't stop him from getting in trouble, though. He was constantly getting picked up for one thing or another. He even did a few weeks in juvie. Eventually the state removed him from the home as a repeat juvenile offender and I tried to forget it ever happened." She shook her head. "I never dreamed he would try to do it again. I feel awful."

"Mrs. Curtis's story was so similar to Julianne's that there was no reason to believe she wasn't telling the truth. The forensic evidence supported her version of his death. There's not a grand jury that would indict her. Anything that happened after the fact is well past the statute of limitations." Pat looked down the hall at the sheriff's office and shook his head. "Sheriff Duke might not be happy, but the only real crime here was committed by the deceased a long time ago. As much as I'd like to, I can't charge a dead man with second-degree sexual assault."

The words hung in the air for a moment. Heath let them sink into his mind. Pat meant *attempted* sexual assault, right? Attempted. Julianne had sworn that Tommy hadn't… And yet, why would a traumatized young girl want to tell him something like that? She wouldn't.

And then it hit him like he'd driven his Porsche into a brick wall. In an instant, every moment made sense. Every reaction Julianne ever had. Their wedding night…

How could he have missed this? It was so obvious now that he felt like a fool. And a first-class ass. He'd believed what she told him despite all the signs indicating otherwise. All these years he'd been angry with her while she'd carried this secret on her own.

"I'm going to have a talk with the local child services agency. There is a major breach in conduct if they didn't share the information about Deborah's assault with Mr. and Mrs. Eden before they placed Tommy there. They might not have taken him in if they'd known." The phone on Pat's hip rang and he looked down at the screen. "If you'll excuse me," he said, disappearing through the double doors.

After a few silent, awkward moments, Deborah spoke again, this time to Julianne. "Mr. Richards and I were listening in the observation room while you told your story," she said. "You are so much braver than I ever could have been. I'm sorry I wasn't stronger. If I had been, I would've pressed charges or talked to people about what happened and this might never have happened to you."

Julianne approached Deborah and embraced her. The two women held each other for a moment. "This is not your fault. Don't you ever think that. I've kept this a secret, too. It's hard to tell people the truth, even though you didn't do anything wrong."

When Julianne pulled away, Deborah dabbed her eyes with a tissue and sniffed. "You know, I came back to Cornwall to track down Tommy, but I wasn't looking for a happy family reunion. My therapist had recommended I find him so I could confront my fears and move on. He had vanished, but I expected him to be in jail or working at a gas station in the middle of nowhere. This," she said, waving her hand around, "was more than I ever planned to uncover. But it's better, I think. I don't have to be afraid of Tommy anymore. He's never going to show up on my doorstep and he'll never be able to hurt me or my little girl. I'm happy I was able to help with your case, too. It makes me feel like I have more power and control over my life than ever before."

Heath stood quietly while the two women spoke. He had so many things he wanted and needed to say to Julianne, but now wasn't the time. They eventually moved down the hallway, making their way out of the police station.

He was relieved to step outside. It was cold, but the sun

was shining. It was like an omen; Noah's rainbow signaling that all of this was finally over. They no longer had to worry about the police coming after them. It was in the past now, where it belonged.

At least most of it. With the truth out, the papers would no doubt pick up the story. They needed to sit down with Mom and Dad and tell them what had happened before some woman cornered Molly at the grocery store. Hopefully Ken's heart could withstand the news now that the threat of his children's incarceration was behind them.

Heath whipped out his phone to text his brothers, but found that wasn't enough. He needed to call them. He and Julianne both, to share the news. He wished he could give Julianne time to prepare, but the truth was out. They had protected her as well as they could over the years, but now she would have to tell her story. First to her family, then to the public. Perhaps after all this time, the blow of it would soften. He couldn't imagine the tiny, thirteen-year-old Julianne talking to police and reporters about killing her attacker. Her *rapist*.

His stomach still ached painfully at that thought. If he had only come across the two of them a few minutes sooner. He might have stopped Tommy before he could have… He sighed and shoved his hands into his pockets. He already believed he failed to protect Julianne, but he had no idea the extent of the damage that was caused. And by keeping Tommy's death a secret, they had virtually forced her to keep the rape a secret as well, and hadn't even known it. Had their attempt to protect her only made it worse?

The bile started to rise in the back of his throat. She should have been taken to the doctor. To a therapist. She should've been able to cry in her mother's arms and she was never able to do any of that.

His knees started to weaken beneath him, so Heath moved quickly to sit on the steps. He would wait there until Julianne and Deborah were done talking. Maybe by then, he could pull himself together.

After a while, Deborah embraced Julianne again, and then she made her way down the sidewalk to her car. Julianne watched her walk away and then finally turned to look at him. It was the first time she'd done that since they'd all gathered inside the police station. She walked over to the steps and sat down beside him.

Minutes passed before either of them spoke. They had shared so much together, and yet when it came to the important things, they knew almost nothing about each other.

"Thank you," she said at last.

That was the last thing he ever expected her to say. "Why on earth would you be thanking me right now?"

"Thank you for loving me," she elaborated. "No matter what we've said or done to each other over the years, when it was important, you were there for me. You probably don't think so, but the truth is that you would have gone to jail for me today. You've spent the last sixteen years covering for me, even lying to your own brothers about what happened that day. You looked Sheriff Duke in the eye and told him you killed Tommy, consequences be damned. How many people are lucky enough to have someone in their life that is willing to do that for them?"

"That's what families do. They protect each other." He watched the traffic drift by the main thoroughfare for a moment. He couldn't turn to face her while he spoke or he might give away the fact that his feelings for her ran much deeper than that. No matter what happened between them, he would always love Julianne. He couldn't seem to stop. Knowing the truth only made it harder not to love her more. All his reasons for keeping her at arm's length were nullified. But they were divorced. What did that matter now?

"You went far beyond family obligation, Heath."

"Why didn't you tell me what happened, Jules? You could've told me the truth."

"No," she said, softly shaking the blond curls around her shoulders. "I couldn't. You had me on this pedestal. I couldn't bear for you to know how flawed I was. How broken I was."

"As though what happened was your fault?"

"It wasn't my fault. I know that. But it wasn't your fault, either. If you knew, you would've blamed yourself. And you'd never look at me the same way again. I didn't want to lose that. You were the only person in my life that made me feel special. Mom and Dad loved me, but I always felt like I wasn't enough for them. You only wanted me. I wanted to stay that perfect vision in your mind."

"By making me despise you? You made me stay up nights wondering what I'd done wrong. Christ, I *divorced* you."

Julianne turned to look at him with a soft smile curling her lips. "I tried to push you away, but you still loved me. All this time, that was the one thing I kept hoping would change. I couldn't tell you the truth, so I knew there would always be a barrier between us. I kept hoping you'd move on and find someone who could love you the way you deserved to be loved. The way you loved me."

He shook his head. He didn't want anyone else to love him. All he had ever wanted was for Julianne to love him. And the way she spoke convinced him that she did. Maybe she had all this time, but the secret she kept was too big. It was easier to keep away than be subjected to his constant needling about why she left him. But to push him into another woman's arms *because* she loved him? "I still don't understand what you're thinking sometimes, Jules."

"I know." She patted his knee and stood up. "Let's go home. We have some long conversations to have with the family."

He got up and followed her to the street. She was right. And he had one important conversation with Ken in mind that she wouldn't be expecting.

Twelve

It was over. Good and truly over.

Julianne slipped into her coat and went out onto the porch to gather herself. The last hour had been harder than confessing the truth to Sheriff Duke. Looking her parents in the eye and telling them everything had been excruciating. Not for her, but she hated to burden them with the truth.

They had taken it better than she expected. Ken got quiet and shook his head, but his color was good and he remained stable. When it was over he'd hugged her tighter than he'd ever hugged her in her entire life. Molly cried a lot. Julianne expected that she would continue to for a while. Her mother was a mother hen. Knowing that had happened to her children under her watch would eat at her for a long time. Maybe always. But Julianne assured her that she was okay, it was a long time ago, and it seemed to calm her.

As she stepped onto the gravel lot behind the house, Julianne looked out at the trees. She had loved being out there once but hadn't set foot in the fields in sixteen years. The boogeyman was long gone. Most of her own personal demons had been set loose today. She took a deep breath and headed for the north field. That was where she'd been that day. If she were going to face this, she needed to go there.

It didn't take long to find the spot, but it took a while to walk out there. The trees were different, always changing as they were harvested and replanted. There were no monsters in the trees, no men to chase her, but she could feel the change in the weight on her chest as she got closer. While Wade had hidden the body and Brody took her to shower and change, Heath and Xander had cleaned up the scene. The rock she'd hit him with was flung into the far reaches of the property. The pool of blood was long gone. But when she looked, she could still see it all.

That's when the first snowflake drifted past her face. One flake became ten, became a thousand. In only a few minutes' time, the tree branches were dusted with white and the bloodstain in her mind slowly disappeared beneath a layer of snow.

It was a perfect moment. A pure, white cleansing of her past. She tipped her face up, feeling the tiny prickles of flakes melting on her cheeks, and sucked in a deep, cold breath.

Over.

Julianne turned her back to the scene of her attack, putting it behind her with everything else, and started walking in the opposite direction, through the fields. For the first time since she was thirteen, she could enjoy the moment. The snow was beautiful, drifting slowly down into fluffy clumps on the branches. The flakes were getting fatter, some larger than nickels. They would have several inches sticking before too long.

She climbed up the slope of the back property, looking for her favorite place on the farm. Somehow she expected it to have changed, but when she finally reached it, everything was just as she remembered. There, jutting out of the side of the hill, was a large, flat rock. She had come out here to sit and think when she was younger. The household was always full of kids and this was a place she could be alone.

Julianne dusted off the snow and sat down on the rock, turning to face the slope of the property laid out in front of her. To the left, she could see the roofline and lights of Wade and Tori's house over the hill. In front of her was the whole of the Garden of Eden. Her own little paradise.

It was nearing sunset, but the fat, gray clouds blocked out the color of the sky. The light was fading, but she could still make out the rows of trees stretching in front of her. The big house, with glowing windows and black smoke rising from the chimney, lay beyond it. Then the dark shape of the bunkhouse with Heath's silver Porsche out front.

Heath. Her ex-husband. Julianne sighed and snuggled deeper into her coat. With Sheriff Duke's unexpected arrival, she hadn't had much time to process her new marital status. While they had come clean about Tommy, they had deliberately opted not to tell anyone about the marriage. That was too much for one day. It might not be something they ever needed to tell. What would it matter, really? It only impacted the two of them since they were the only ones aware of it. And since it was done…it would only hurt her family to find out now.

But, like anything else in her life, keeping her feelings inside made it harder to deal with it.

Maybe if she hadn't come back to stay in Cornwall she

would feel differently about her freedom. If she hadn't made love to him. If they hadn't gone to Paris together. If the last month and a half never happened she might feel relieved and ready to move on her with life.

But it *had* happened. She had let herself get closer to Heath than she ever had in the eleven years of their marriage and then it was all done. How was she supposed to just walk away? How was she going to learn to stop loving him? Eleven years apart hadn't done it. Was she doomed to another eleven years of quiet pining for him?

In the gathering darkness, Julianne noticed a dancing light coming up the main tree lane from the house. The snow had let up a little, making it easier to see the figure was walking toward her with a flashlight. She tensed. She was at a tentative truce with the trees, but she wasn't sure if adding another person would work. It didn't feel as secure as being here alone.

Then she made out the distinctive bright blue of the coat and realized it was Heath. She sighed. Why had he followed her out here? She needed some time alone to mourn their relationship and deal with a hellish day.

Heath stopped a few feet short of the rock, not crowding into her space. "Your rock has missed you."

At that Julianne chuckled. Even Heath remembered how much time she had spent sitting in this very spot when they were kids. "Fortunately, time is relative to a rock."

"I still feel bad for it. I know I couldn't go that long without you in my life."

The light atmosphere between then shifted. Her gaze lifted to meet his, her smile fading. "Life doesn't always work out the way you plan. Even for a rock."

"I disagree. Life might throw obstacles in your path, but if you want something with your whole heart and soul, you have to fight for it. Nothing that's easy is worth having and nothing worth having is easy. You, Julianne, have been incredibly difficult."

"I'm going to take that as a compliment."

He smiled. "You should. I meant it as one. You're worth every moment of pain and frustration and confusion I've gone through. And I think, perhaps, that we might have weathered the trials. In every fairy tale, the prince and the maiden have obstacles to triumph over and strengthen their love. I think the evil villain has been defeated. I'm ready for the happy ending."

It sounded good. Really, it did. But so much had happened. Could they really ever get back to a happy ending? "Life isn't a fairy tale, Heath. We're divorced. I've never read a story where the prince and his princess divorce."

"Yeah, but they have angry dragons and evil wizards. I'll take a divorce any day because things can always change. We don't have to stay divorced. We can slay this dragon, if you're willing to face it with me."

She watched as his hand slipped into his coat pocket and retrieved a small box. A jewelry box. Her heart stilled in her chest. What was he doing? They'd been divorced for two days. He wasn't really…he couldn't possibly want this after everything that had happened.

"Heath…" she began.

"Let me say what I need to say," he insisted. "When we were eighteen, we got married for all the wrong reasons. We loved each other but we were young and stupid. We didn't think it through. Life is complicated and we were unprepared for the reality of it. But I also think we got divorced for all the wrong reasons."

Heath crouched down at the foot of the rock, looking up at her. "I love you. I've always loved you. I never imagined my life or my future without you in it. I was hurt that you wouldn't open up to me and I used our divorce to punish you for it. Now, I understand why you held back. And I realized that everything you did that hurt me was also meant to somehow protect me.

"You said at the police station today that I was willing to go to jail for you. And you were right. I was willing to take on years of misery behind bars to protect you. Just as you were willing to give me a divorce and face a future alone in the hopes that I could find someone to make me happy."

"That's not the same," she insisted.

"A self-imposed prison is just as difficult to escape as one of iron and stone, Jules." He held up the box and looked her square in the eye. "Consider this a jailbreak."

"Are you honestly telling me that between Parisian jet lag, getting divorced, getting arrested and spending all day at the police station, you had the time to go to the jeweler and buy an engagement ring?"

"No," he said.

Julianne instantly felt foolish. Had she misinterpreted the whole thing? If there were earrings in that box she would feel like an idiot. "Then what is going on? If you're not proposing, what are you doing?"

"I am proposing. But you asked if I went to a jeweler and I didn't. I went to talk to Ken."

Julianne swallowed hard. "We agreed we weren't going to tell them about us."

"Correction. We agreed not to tell them we were married before. You said nothing about telling him that I was in love with you and wanted his blessing to marry you. No one needs to know it's round two for us."

She winced, torn between her curiosity about what was in the box, her elation about his confession of love and how her daddy had taken the news. "What happened?" she asked.

Heath smiled wide, easing her concerns. "He asked me

what the hell had taken so long. And then he gave me this."
He opened the hinge on the box to reveal the ring inside.

It couldn't be. Julianne's jaw dropped open. The large round diamond, the eight diamonds encircling it, the intricate gold lacework of the dull, worn band... It was her grandmother's wedding ring. She hadn't seen this ring since she was a small child and Nanna was still alive.

Heath pulled the ring from the box and held it up to her. "The last ring I gave you was cheap and ugly. This time, I have enough money to buy you any ring you'd like, but I wanted a ring that meant something. Ken told me that they had been saving this ring in the hopes that one day it would be your engagement ring. He knew how much you loved your nanna and thought this would be perfect. I was inclined to agree.

"Julianne Eden, will you marry me *again?*"

Heath was kneeling in the snow, freezing and holding his breath. Julianne took far too long to answer. Her expression changed faster than he could follow. At first, she'd stared at that ring like he was holding up a severed head. Then her expression softened and she seemed on the verge of tears. After that, she'd gone stony and silent. Waiting more than a beat or two to answer a question like this was really bad form.

"Yes."

And then his heart leapt in his chest. "Yes?"

Julianne smiled, her eyes brimming with tears. "Yes, I will marry you again."

Heath scrambled to slip the ring onto her finger. It flopped around a bit. "I'm sorry it's too big. We'll get it sized down as soon as we can get to a jeweler."

"That's okay. Nanna was Daddy's mother and I take after Mama's side of the family. We're much tinier people." She looked down at the ring and her face was nearly beaming. "I love it. It's more than perfect."

She lunged forward into his arms, knocking him backward into the snow. Before he knew it, he was lying in the cold fluff and Julianne was on top of him, kissing him. Not so bad, after all. He ignored the cold, focusing on the taste of the lips he'd thought he might never kiss again. That was enough to warm his blood and chase off any chill.

Julianne was going to marry him. That just left telling Molly. Even though he now knew that Julianne had never kept their relationship a secret out of embarrassment, the idea shouldn't bother him, but he still felt a nervous tremble in his stomach. A part of him was afraid to say the words. "It's getting dark. Are you ready to head back to the house and tell everyone?"

He expected her to dodge the way she always did, to make some excuse, to say that she wanted to celebrate with just the two of them for now. A part of him would even understand if she wanted to wait until tomorrow after all the drama of the day.

"Absolutely," she said, smiling down at him. "I'm thrilled to give them some good news for a change."

Relief flooded through him, and the last barrier to total bliss was gone. They got up and held hands as they walked back through the trees to the house. When they came in together through the back door, Molly was in the kitchen cooking and Ken was in the living room reading a book.

"Mom, do you have a minute?"

Molly nodded, more focused on the boiling of her potatoes than the clasping of their hands. "Yes, these need to go for a bit longer."

"Come into the living room," Heath said, herding her ahead of them to sit down next to Ken by the fireplace.

Heath and Julianne sat opposite them. He was still holding Julianne's hand for support. She leaned into him, placing her left hand over their clasped ones and inadvertently displaying her ring.

"Mom, Dad..." Heath began.

"What is that?" Molly asked, her eyes glued on Julianne's hand. "Is that an engagement ring? Wait. Is that Nanna's ring?" She turned to Ken with an accusatory glare. "You knew about this and you didn't tell me!"

Ken shrugged. If he got wound up every time Molly did, he would have had twenty heart attacks by now. "He asked for my blessing, so I gave him the ring. That's what you wanted, didn't you? Saving the ring for Jules was your idea."

"Of course it's what I wanted." Molly's emotions seemed to level out as she realized she should be more focused on the fact that Heath and Julianne were engaged. A bright smile lit her face. "My baby is getting married!" She leapt from her chair and gathered Julianne into her arms.

She tugged Heath up from his seat to hug him next. "I didn't even know you two were seeing each other," she scolded. "A heads-up would have been nice before you dropped a marriage bomb on me! Lordy, so much news today. Is there anything else you all need to tell us?"

Heath stiffened in her arms. He was never good at lying to Molly, but Julianne was adamant that their prior marriage stay quiet, no matter what. "Isn't this enough?" he said with a smile.

"Wonderful news," Molly said, her eyes getting misty and far off as her mind drifted. "We'll have the wedding here at the farm," she declared. "It will be beautiful. Everyone in town will want to come. Please don't tell me you want a small affair or destination wedding in Antigua."

Julianne smiled and patted Molly's shoulder. "We'll

have it here, I promise. And it can be as big and fabulous as you can imagine it."

"This time," Heath added, "I think we need to have a grand wedding with the big cake and a swing band."

"This time?" Molly said, her brow furrowed.

Julianne turned to look at him, her green eyes wide with silent condemnation. It wasn't until then that Heath fully realized what he'd said. Damn it. With a shake of her head, Julianne held out her hand, gesturing for him to spill the last of their secrets. They might as well.

"Uh, Mom…" he began. "Julianne and I, uh, eloped when we were eighteen."

Both he and Julianne took a large step backward out of the blast zone. Molly's eyes grew wide, but before she could open her mouth, Ken stood up and clasped her shoulders tightly. It made Heath wonder if it was Ken's subtle restraining of his tiny wife hidden beneath the guise of supportiveness.

Molly's mouth opened, then closed as she took a deep breath to collect her thoughts. "When did this happen?"

"While we were on our European vacation after graduation."

"You two immediately went off to separate schools when you got home," she said with a frown.

"Yeah, we didn't plan that well," Heath admitted. Even if they'd had the perfect honeymoon and had come home blissfully in love they still would have faced the huge obstacles of where they went from there. They were heading to different schools a thousand miles apart. Not exactly the best way to start a marriage, but an ideal way to start a trial separation.

"And how long were you two married? I'm assuming you're divorced now, considering you're engaged again."

This time Heath looked at Julianne. It was her turn to

fess up since they were married that long due to her own procrastination.

"Eleven years. Our divorce was final a couple days ago."

Molly closed her eyes. "I'm not going to ask. I really don't think I want to know. You think you know what's going on in your kids' lives, but you have no clue. You two were married this whole time. Xander and Rose had a baby I never knew about. And to think I believed all of you were too busy with careers and I might never see everyone settled down!"

"We would've told you, Mama, but we pretty much broke up right after we married. We've been separated all this time."

"I think I've had about all the news I can take for one day, good or bad. This calls for a pot of tea, I think. You can let go of me now, Ken." Molly headed for the kitchen, then stopped in the entryway. "I might as well ask…you're not pregnant, are you?"

Julianne shook her head adamantly. "No, Mama. I promise we are not pregnant."

"All right," she said. "You two wash up. It's almost time for supper."

Molly disappeared. Ken clapped Heath on the shoulder as he passed by. In a moment, they were alone with all their secrets out on the table.

"I think it was better this way, don't you?" Heath asked.

"You only think that because you're the one that spilled the beans."

Heath turned to her and pulled Julianne into his arms. "Maybe. But I am happy to start our new life together with no more secrets. Everything is out in the open at last. Right? You've told me all of it?"

Julianne nodded, climbing to her toes to place a kiss on his lips. "Of course, dear."

Heath laughed. "Spoken like a wife filled with secrets she keeps from her husband."

She wrapped her arms around his neck, a naughty grin curling her lips as she looked up at him. "This *is* my second marriage, you'll remember. I'm an old pro at this now."

"Don't think I don't know all your tricks, woman. It's my second marriage, too," Heath noted. "And last."

Julianne smiled. "It better be."

Epilogue

It was a glorious spring day in northwestern Connecticut. The sun was shining on the farm. The delicate centerpieces of roses, hydrangeas, lilies and orchids were warming in the afternoon light, emitting a soft fragrance on the breeze. It was the perfect day for a wedding on the farm; the second in the last six months, with two more on the horizon.

Molly was absolutely beaming. She'd been waiting years to see her children marry and start families of their own. All of them had been more focused on careers than romance, much to her chagrin, but things had turned around and fast. It seemed like each of them had gone from single to engaged in the blink of an eye.

Today was Brody and Samantha's big day. It was the ceremony that she'd lain awake nights worrying she might never see. Molly had always hoped that Brody would find a woman who could look beyond the scars. She couldn't have imagined a more perfect match for him than Sam.

She had thought for certain that Brody and Sam would opt for a wedding in Boston. He'd promised her a huge ceremony with half the eastern seaboard in attendance, but when it came down to it, Sam had wanted something far more intimate at the farm, which thrilled Molly. That didn't mean a simple affair, by any stretch—this was still Sam's wedding they were talking about. Her new daughter-in-law imagined an event that was pink and covered in flowers and Swarovski crystals.

All of "her girls" were so different, and Molly was so pleased to be able to finally say that. She had four daughters now, and each of their weddings would be unique experiences that would keep the farm hopping all year.

When Ken had his heart attack, Wade and Tori had postponed their plans for a fall wedding. Since Brody and Sam were already planning a spring ceremony, they opted to wait until the following autumn and keep with the rustic theme they'd designed. Xander and Rose were marrying over the long Fourth of July weekend in an appropriately patriotic extravaganza.

And as for Heath and Julianne…they hadn't gotten very far into planning their second wedding when it all got chucked out the window. They'd promised Molly a big ceremony, but when they realized they'd come home from Paris with more than just souvenirs, they moved up the timeline.

Molly stepped away from her duties as mother of the groom to search for her daughter in the crowd. Julianne was sitting beneath the shade of the tent, absent-mindedly stroking her round, protruding belly. The delicate pink bridesmaid gown Sam had selected for her daughter to wear did little to hide the fact that she was extremely pregnant. Although Julianne had sworn she had no more secrets, in only two months, Molly would be holding her second grandbaby and she could hardly wait.

Julianne and Heath had had the first of the weddings on the farm—a small family ceremony while everyone was home for Christmas. It was the polar opposite of today's circus. Brody and Sam had a band, dancing, and a catered sit-down meal.

A new song began and Brody led Sam onto the dance floor. They might as well have been the only people here since Brody couldn't take his eyes off of her. His bride was beaming like a ray of sunshine. Her white satin gown was stunning against the golden tan of her skin. The intricate crystal and bead work traveled down the bodice to the mermaid skirt, highlighting every amazing curve of Sam's body. Her veil was long, flowing down her back to pool on the parquet dance floor they set up on the lawn. She was stunning.

Brody, too, was looking handsome. Molly had always thought he was a good-looking boy, but the first round of reconstructive surgery with the specialist had done wonders for his scars. There would be more surgeries in the future, but Molly could already see the dramatic change in the way he carried himself. She'd never seen Brody look happier than he did right now.

It wasn't long before Wade and Tori joined them on the dance floor. Then Xander and Rose. Julianne took a little convincing, but eventually Heath lured her out to dance, completing the wedding party.

The sight of all of them together brought a happy tear to Molly's eye. The last few years had been so hard with nearly losing Ken, the crippling financial burden of his medical bills and dealing with the police investigation. Even when all that was behind them, Molly and Ken had to work through their guilt over what had happened with

Tommy and how their children had suffered silently for all these years. It had been rough, but the Edens were made of stern stuff and they had survived and become stronger for it. The year of weddings at the Garden of Eden was a fresh start for the whole family.

Molly felt a warmth at her back, then the slide of Ken's arms around her waist. He hugged her to his chest, pressing a kiss against her cheek.

"Look at our beautiful family, Mama," he whispered into her ear.

Molly relished the feel of his still strong arms holding her and sighed with contentment. "It's hard to believe there was a time we thought we might not have any children," she said. "And here we are with a full house. And grandbabies."

"It's better than I ever imagined or could even have hoped for. I think the fairy tale I promised you on our wedding day is finally complete."

"Yes," Molly agreed. "We've reached our happily ever after."

* * * * *

If you loved HER SECRET HUSBAND,
pick up the other stories in the
SECRETS OF EDEN *series from*
Andrea Laurence:

UNDENIABLE DEMANDS
A BEAUTY UNCOVERED
HEIR TO SCANDAL

Available now from Harlequin Desire!

REQUEST YOUR FREE BOOKS!
2 FREE NOVELS PLUS 2 FREE GIFTS!

◆HARLEQUIN® *Desire*

ALWAYS POWERFUL, PASSIONATE AND PROVOCATIVE

YES! Please send me 2 FREE Harlequin Desire® novels and my 2 FREE gifts (gifts are worth about $10). After receiving them, if I don't wish to receive any more books, I can return the shipping statement marked "cancel." If I don't cancel, I will receive 6 brand-new novels every month and be billed just $4.55 per book in the U.S. or $4.99 per book in Canada. That's a savings of at least 13% off the cover price! It's quite a bargain! Shipping and handling is just 50¢ per book in the U.S. and 75¢ per book in Canada.* I understand that accepting the 2 free books and gifts places me under no obligation to buy anything. I can always return a shipment and cancel at any time. Even if I never buy another book, the two free books and gifts are mine to keep forever.

225/326 HDN F4ZC

Name _____ (PLEASE PRINT) _____

Address _____ Apt. #

City _____ State/Prov. _____ Zip/Postal Code

Signature (if under 18, a parent or guardian must sign)

Mail to the **Harlequin® Reader Service:**

IN U.S.A.: P.O. Box 1867, Buffalo, NY 14240-1867
IN CANADA: P.O. Box 609, Fort Erie, Ontario L2A 5X3

Want to try two free books from another line?
Call 1-800-873-8635 or visit www.ReaderService.com.

* Terms and prices subject to change without notice. Prices do not include applicable taxes. Sales tax applicable in N.Y. Canadian residents will be charged applicable taxes. Offer not valid in Quebec. This offer is limited to one order per household. Not valid for current subscribers to Harlequin Desire books. All orders subject to credit approval. Credit or debit balances in a customer's account(s) may be offset by any other outstanding balance owed by or to the customer. Please allow 4 to 6 weeks for delivery. Offer available while quantities last.

Your Privacy—The Harlequin® Reader Service is committed to protecting your privacy. Our Privacy Policy is available online at www.ReaderService.com or upon request from the Harlequin Reader Service.

We make a portion of our mailing list available to reputable third parties that offer products we believe may interest you. If you prefer that we not exchange your name with third parties, or if you wish to clarify or modify your communication preferences, please visit us at www.ReaderService.com/consumerschoice or write to us at Harlequin Reader Service Preference Service, P.O. Box 9062, Buffalo, NY 14269. Include your complete name and address.

HD13R

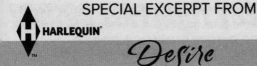
Here's a sneak peek at the next scandalous Beaumont Heirs book,

A BEAUMONT CHRISTMAS WEDDING
By Sarah M. Anderson

Available November 2014 from Harlequin® Desire.

What if Matthew Beaumont could look at her without caring about who she'd been in the past?

What if—what if he wasn't involved with anyone?

Whitney didn't hook up. That part of her life was dead and buried. But…a little Christmas romance between the maid of honor and the best man wouldn't be such a bad thing, would it? It could be fun.

She hurried to the bathroom, daring to hope that Matthew was single. He was coming to dinner tonight and it sounded as if he would be involved with a lot of the wedding activities.

Although…it had been a long time since she'd attempted anything involving the opposite sex. Making a pass at the best man might not be the smartest thing she could do.

Even so, Whitney went with the red cashmere sweater—the kind a single, handsome man might accidentally brush with his fingers—and headed out. The house had hallways in all directions, and she was relieved when she heard voices—Jo's and Phillip's and another voice, deep and strong. Matthew.

She hurried down the steps, then remembered she was trying to make a good impression. She slowed too quickly and stumbled. Hard. She braced for the impact.

It didn't come. Instead of hitting the floor, she fell into a pair of strong arms and against a firm, warm chest.

Whitney looked up into a pair of eyes that were deep blue. He smiled down at her and she didn't feel as if she was going to forget her own name. She felt as if she'd never forget this moment.

"I've got you."

He did have her. His arms were around her waist and he was lifting her up. She felt secure.

The feeling was *wonderful.*

Then, without warning, everything changed. His warm smile froze as his eyes went hard. The strong arms became iron bars around her and the next thing she knew, she was being pushed not up, but away.

Matthew Beaumont set her back on her feet and stepped clear of her. With a glare that could only be described as ferocious, he turned to Phillip and Jo.

"What," he said, "is Whitney Wildz doing here?"

Don't miss
A BEAUMONT CHRISTMAS WEDDING
By Sarah M. Anderson

Available November 2014 from Harlequin® Desire.

HARLEQUIN®

Desire

POWERFUL HEROES... SCANDALOUS SECRETS... BURNING DESIRES!

**Explore the new tantalizing story from
the *Texas Cattleman's Club: After the Storm* series**

SHELTERED BY THE MILLIONAIRE

by *USA TODAY* bestselling author
Catherine Mann

As a Texas town rebuilds, love heals all wounds....

Texas tycoon Drew Farrell has always been a thorn in
Beth Andrews's side, especially when he puts the kibosh
on her animal shelter. But when he saves her daughter
during the worst tornado in recent memory, Beth sees
beneath his prickly exterior to the hero underneath.
Soon, the storm's recovery makes bedfellows of these
opposites. Until Beth's old reflexes kick in—should she
brace for betrayal or say yes to Drew once and for all?

Available ***NOVEMBER 2014***
wherever books and ebooks are sold.

Talk to us online!
www.Facebook.com/HarlequinBooks
www.Pinterest.com/HarlequinBooks
www.Twitter.com/HarlequinBooks

HD733491

HARLEQUIN®

Desire

POWERFUL HEROES... SCANDALOUS SECRETS... BURNING DESIRES!

THE COWBOY'S PRIDE AND JOY

by *USA TODAY* bestselling author
Maureen Child

Available November 2014

A cowboy gets a baby surprise in this new novel from Harlequin Desire's Billionaires & Babies collection!

All former soldier Jake Hunter wants is peace and quiet. But when his Boston blueblood mother sends her assistant Cassidy Moore to see him on family business, chaos ensues. Their attraction rages out of control as a snowstorm strands them on his Montana ranch.

Flash-forward nine months: Cassie can't bring herself to tell Jake she's had his child. But when his mother interferes again, Cassie rushes back to Jake... just in time for another blizzard, and the Christmas spirit, to open one reclusive cowboy's heart.

This exciting new story is part of Harlequin® Desire's popular *Billionaires & Babies* collection featuring powerful men...wrapped around their babies' little fingers!

Available wherever books and ebooks are sold.

HD73348